A PSALMIST CALLED ASAPH

THE CALLED
BOOK 12

KENNETH A. WINTER

WildernessLessons

JOIN MY READERS' GROUP FOR UPDATES AND FUTURE RELEASES

Please join my Readers' Group so i can send you a free book, as well as updates and information about future releases, etc.

See the back of the book for details on how to sign up.

A Psalmist Called Asaph

The Called – Book 12 (a series of novellas)

Published by:

Kenneth A. Winter

WildernessLessons, LLC

Richmond, Virginia

United States of America

kenwinter.org

wildernesslessons.com

Edited by Sheryl Martin Hash

Cover design by Scott Campbell Design

ISBN 978-1-9568664-0-7(soft cover)

ISBN 978-1-9568664-1-4(e-book)

ISBN 978-1-9568664-2-1 (large print)

Library of Congress Control Number: 2025901619

The basis for the story line of this book is taken from *the Books of First Samuel, Second Samuel, First Kings and Psalms* in the Holy Bible. Certain fictional events or depictions of those events have been added.

DEDICATION

This book is dedicated to two very special people, without whom it never would have been written.

The first—my friend, my pastor, and one who has been faithful to speak a word fitly into my ear, even when he didn't realize he was doing so. His name is Christopher (Chris) Barras.

Chris is the Lead Elder and Minister of Area 10 Faith Community in Richmond, Virginia, having planted the church sixteen years ago.

In the early phase of this book, i was asking the Lord to show me the next character on which to base the final story of **The Called** *series. My intent was to keep the twelve books – equal representations of both the Old Testament and New Testament.*

My remaining book needed a hero from the Old Testament. As my wife and i entered into the worship service one morning, i realized that all the music was being taken from three of the Books of Psalms. As Chris stood to speak, he mentioned that those three psalms, together with others, had all been authored by Asaph.

At that moment, the Holy Spirit confirmed in my heart that Chris had just given me His answer.

The second dedicatee of this book is my friend, Sheryl Martin Hash.

As most of you know by now, Sheryl has been the editor of all my biblical fiction novels, novellas, and short stories, as well as my two recent contemporary Christian novels. She knows my writing style better than anyone else , and in the background has always been able to help me write a better book.

i have recently been diagnosed with metastatic lung cancer, which, together with an inoperable mass on my lung, has spread lesions to my brain, spine, and other parts of my body. These are now affecting my cognitive abilities. i have asked Sheryl to oversee the final draft of my manuscript, improve it through needed script enhancements, and edit to improve its overall flow. i trust that together we will produce the kind of book you have come to love and appreciate from us.

Thank you both for the invaluable contributions you have made!

∾

CONTENTS

PREFACE

~

This fictional novella is the final book in the series titled, *The Called*. Like the others, it is a story about an ordinary person who surrendered his life to God and was called by Him to be used in extraordinary ways. As i've said in my previous books, we tend to elevate the people we read about in Scripture and place them on a pedestal far beyond our reach because of the faith they exhibited. But Asaph, perhaps more obscure in Scripture than others, shows us a flawed human being who could never have accomplished on his own what God did through him.

Even though generations have come and gone, Asaph's name has not been forgotten. His music, his faith, and his psalms have endured through the ages and have been sung by the people of Israel in times of joy and sorrow, prosperity and exile.

Even as the kingdom of Israel fractured and the people were scattered, the psalms of Asaph rose from the hearts of the faithful. His lament for the state of Israel, his trust in the promises of Jehovah God, and his hope for the future lived on in the worship of God's people. For though Asaph was gone, the God he served remained, and His promises would never fail.

Followers of Christ continue to read and sing the psalms of Asaph today (Psalms 50 and 73-83). A unique and powerful collection, they reflect a life of deep spiritual insights, vivid imagery, and passionate pleas for divine justice. The undercurrent within his soul over the apparent prosperity of the wicked and the eventual triumph of righteousness unfolded in his life as well as in his songs.

His story in many ways is similar to each one of ours. His life was etched by his experiences, both good and bad—by the victories and the defeats, as well as the positive and negative influences in his life.

His storyline is extracted from the books of First Samuel, Second Samuel, and First Kings, as well as from the Psalms he penned.

In writing this book, i have taken what we know about Asaph from Scripture and historical records and crafted a plausible story of what his life and relationships with David and Solomon might have been. So, i invite you to join Asaph as he shares his unique journey and his interaction with two of the greatest kings of Israel. You will also recognize other individuals mentioned in the story; i have created background details for some so we might better see them as people and not just names.

i have also added several fictional characters to round out the story, plus i have given names to those we know existed but remained unnamed in the Bible. They represent people who would have surrounded Asaph during his lifetime. Included as an appendix in the back of this book is a character listing to clarify the historical vs. fictional elements of each character.

Whenever i directly quote Scripture, it is italicized and includes a super-script number. The Scripture references are also included as an appendix in the book. The remaining instances of dialogue not italicized are a part of the fictional story that helps advance the narrative.

My hope is this book will prompt you to reread the biblical account of Asaph's life and the events surrounding it. You will be reminded of how God worked through this ordinary man to accomplish His extraordinary purpose. None of my books is intended to be a substitute for God's Word; rather, i hope they will lead you to spend more time in His Word.

Finally, my prayer is you will see Asaph through fresh eyes and be challenged to live out *your* walk with the Lord with the same conviction, courage, and faith he displayed. And most importantly, i pray you will be challenged to be an "ordinary" follower with the willingness and faith to be used by God in extraordinary ways—to impact not only this generation, but also the generations to come … until our Lord returns!

∾

1

THE ARK OF GOD

~

I stared down at Uzzah's crumpled body. Moments earlier, we had all been singing and dancing before the Lord, joyfully accompanying the Ark of God on its long-overdue journey to Jerusalem. It was a day filled with thanksgiving and celebration—even our king danced in praise to the Lord.

But suddenly, one of the oxen pulling the cart lost its footing on the rocky path. The cart lurched, and the Ark was about to topple to the ground. Uzzah, standing closest to the danger, instinctively reached out his hand to steady the Ark. Any of us would have done the same.

However, the moment his hand touched the Ark, he fell to the ground. I rushed to his side, but it was too late. Though the Ark was safe, Uzzah was dead. A pall fell over us all. What had just happened?

King David looked horrified as he knelt beside Uzzah's body. His lips trembled when he gazed at me, his eyes questioning. I solemnly shook my head.

Breaking the silence, the king cried out, his voice quivering: "God, why have You killed this man? He was only trying to protect Your Ark. Why has Your anger fallen upon him?"

The wind rustled through the valley, but the heavens remained silent.

"Why has this man paid the price for the sins of others?" the king continued. "He was helping return Your Ark to its rightful place. How can I ever bring the Ark into my care now?"

The men around us shifted uneasily, their joy turned to dread. I felt my own faith waver in that moment, a question echoing within: *Had we made a mistake?*

~

It had been a beautiful spring day. The winter barley harvest was approaching, and six months had passed since our king moved his throne from Hebron to Jerusalem following his conquest of the Jebusites. He knew Jerusalem would make a fine capital for the united kingdom of Israel, but there was one thing the city still lacked—the presence of Jehovah God.

After the Israelites left Egypt, Jehovah God had instructed Moses, *"I want the people of Israel to build Me a sacred residence where I can live among them. You must make this Tabernacle and its furnishings exactly according to the plans I will show you."*[1]

So the Israelites had constructed the Ark of the Covenant, a sacred chest that would serve as a physical representation of God's presence among them and where God met with Moses to give His commands for the people.

The Ark's magnificence was something to behold. It was made of acacia wood, overlaid with pure gold inside and out. Bezalel, a skilled craftsman, made it according to the detailed instructions Jehovah gave while the Israelites camped at the foot of Mount Sinai during the first year of their exodus from Egypt.

Poles could be inserted through golden rings at each corner to carry the Ark, and God gave explicit instructions about how and by whom it was to be transported. The chest housed two stone tablets on which God had written the Ten Commandments.

The Ark's cover, called the Mercy Seat, was made of pure gold with a cherub at either end, also of hammered gold. Their wings stretched toward each other, touching at the center. It was here, between the cherubim, that the Lord God Almighty enthroned Himself when the Ark was placed in the Tabernacle.

Priests had carried the Ark before the Israelites into the Jordan River as they crossed into the Promised Land, and for seven days as they marched around Jericho's walls, signifying that God alone was their Deliverer. Even Israel's enemies understood the Ark's significance.

When the sons of Eli, the High Priest, presumptuously took the Ark into battle against the Philistines without seeking the Lord's guidance, they were both killed and the Ark was captured. The wife of Phinehas, one of the two foolish priests, declared, *"The glory has departed from Israel, for the Ark of God has been captured."* [2]

The Ark remained in the possession of the Philistines for seven months. During that time it was placed in three cities—Ashdod, Gath, and Ekron—and in each one the people were afflicted with a plague of tumors that led to death. Ultimately, the Philistines cried out for the Ark to be returned to Israel.

At the instruction of their priests and diviners, the Philistines built a new cart to transport the Ark. Also on the cart was a chest containing an offering of gold in the shape of five tumors and five rats. The cart was drawn by two cows that had never been yoked but were allowed to go wherever they wanted. The cows made their way to the Israelite city of Beth-shemesh. But when seventy men from the city dared to look inside the Ark, Jehovah struck them down.

A cry arose from Judah: *"Who is able to stand in the presence of the Lord, this holy God? Where can we send the Ark from here?"*[3]

The men of Kiriath-jearim took the Ark to the hillside home of Abinadab, whose son Eleazar was appointed its caretaker. There it remained for over eighty years, while all Israel mourned the absence of God's presence. But it was not Jehovah who had abandoned His people; rather, they had turned away from Him, worshiping foreign gods like Ashtoreth and Baal. Yet in His mercy, the Lord raised up Samuel to be His prophet and judge over Israel.

During Samuel's time, the people cried out for a king. David, my king, became Israel's second monarch. Much of my story centers around how he became my friend, and how my friend became my king. But first, I must continue with my story about that fateful day.

It was meant to be a day of great celebration—the Ark of God was finally being brought to the heart of the united kingdom, Jerusalem. The presence of Jehovah would once again dwell among His people.

My king gathered 30,000 of his finest men and led them to the house of Abinadab, who had passed away years earlier. Eleazar, now an old man, advised the king to transport the Ark the same way the Philistines had—on a cart. None of us knew differently, so we followed his advice.

Eleazar's grandsons lifted the Ark onto a new cart yoked to two oxen that had never pulled a cart. Ahio and Uzzah, two of Eleazar's grandsons, guided the oxen, one walking ahead and the other alongside the cart.

King David, wearing a sleeveless garment called a priestly ephod, followed behind, dancing and singing before the Lord.

"Asaph, my friend, this is one of the greatest honors of my life—this sense of being close to the presence of Jehovah God," he had confided earlier.

I, too, felt joyful as I played my lyre, walking alongside the other musicians. The air was filled with music—songs accompanied by harps, tambourines, castanets, and cymbals echoed through the valley.

The sun blazed high in the sky as we neared the halfway point of our journey. The king spotted a threshing floor ahead, offering shade and water, and directed Ahio and Uzzah to turn there. It was then the oxen stumbled and the tragedy unfolded before us.

King David was so overcome with grief that he left the Ark at the threshing floor under the care of Obed-edom, its owner. The king's general soon announced we would return to Jerusalem while Ahio took his brother's body back home. We should reach our destinations by nightfall.

I asked the king for permission to accompany Ahio, along with six others, on the grave journey. We traveled in silence, each of us burdened with the same question: *Why had God done this?*

Ahio broke the stillness, his voice thick with pain. "He was my brother. He only meant to protect the Ark."

"He was brave," I replied softly. "He did what any of us might have done, Ahio."

Another man spoke in a low voice. "I don't understand. Why did God take him? We were honoring Him, bringing the Ark home."

Ahio stopped in his tracks and looked back at the Ark, now barely visible on the horizon. "Perhaps … we did something wrong," he whispered, almost to himself. "But what? What could we have done differently?"

∾

No one had an answer. We quietly continued our journey, each man haunted by his own questions, our hearts joined in sorrow.

∾

2

THE DAYS OF THE JUDGES

~

*G*rowing up, I never tired of hearing stories about my family. I am a son of Levi and a descendant of his son Gershon. Often, the storyteller would pause as he reminisced, letting the weight of each memory settle over my brother and me.

"Your great-grandfather, Michael, like many of your ancestors before him and those since, was raised in the city of Kedesh, one of the refuge cities established by God," he would recount. "He joined the 10,000 fighting men who marched up to Mount Tabor under the leadership of the Naphtalite Barak—who also lived in Kedesh—and Deborah, whom God appointed judge over Israel. As a Levite, your great-grandfather was precluded from fighting, but nothing prevented him from guarding the thresholds of the tents and the luggage.

"Our people had become oppressed under the Hazorite king, Jabin, and his well-trained, well-equipped army. The fighting forces, under the leadership of General Sisera, included 900 iron chariots, 10,000 horsemen, and 300,000 footmen. This was in sharp contrast to the Israelite army of farmers, shepherds, carpenters, and merchants, along with a few Levites on guard duty. They didn't have one chariot, let alone 900, and their horses were used to plowing fields, not engaging in battle.

"Though the Israelites had the element of surprise in their favor when Barak led his men down the slope of Mount Tabor, the odds were still against them. However, Jehovah God used the surprise and resulting chaos to disorient the Hazorite army. They trampled over one another as they retreated with the Israelite warriors in pursuit. The fields were soaked with blood, and by day's end, not a single Hazorite warrior survived."

The one telling the story always concluded by saying, "Amazingly, by God's mercy and grace, only a handful of our warriors died that day, and a surprisingly small number were wounded. God gave us a miraculous victory!

"Sisera somehow escaped, but his fate was soon sealed as he retreated to Hazor. Along the way, he sought shelter in the tent of a Kenite woman named Jael who courageously drove a tent peg through his head while he slept.

"All of Israel was glad about the defeat of the Hazorite warriors at the hands of our fighting men, but they rejoiced and sang songs about Sisera's death at the hands of His champion—Jael—*truly a woman blessed above all women who live in tents!*"[1]

I was told our people lived in peace under Deborah's forty-year rule following the defeat of the Hazorites. My grandfather, Shimea, was born midway during Deborah's rule. Sadly, those years of tranquility lulled our people into a false sense of security. Over time, they again turned their backs on Jehovah God and did evil in His sight, as they had been prone to do in earlier days.

This time, instead of the Hazorites, the Lord allowed a different people to become the enemy who seized their attention. The Midianites had once been allied with the Israelites. Moses's father-in-law, Jethro, had been a prince and priest of Midian; Tzipora, Moses's wife, had been a princess of Midian; and his brother-in-law, Hobab, served as a guide for the Israelites as they wandered through the wilderness. But even before my people had entered into the Promised Land, the Midianites conspired with King Balak of Moab. On the advice of the prophet Balaam, they seduced the Israelites away from Jehovah God through sexual immorality and idolatry.

The Lord directed Moses to take vengeance on the Midianites, resulting in the deaths of all five of their kings as well as the prophet Balaam. The cities of Midian and its citizens were destroyed, except for a remnant of women and girls who were allowed to live. From that remnant, Midian was reborn —with a deep-seated hatred for our people.

By the time of Deborah's death, the Midianites had multiplied into a mighty people who sought to avenge the annihilation of their forebearers. In fact, they were so cruel the Israelites made hiding places for themselves in the mountains and caves. Whenever the Israelites planted crops, Midianite marauders would destroy them.

They left the Israelites with nothing to eat, taking all the sheep, goats, cattle, and donkeys. The enemy horde, along with their livestock and tents, were as thick as locusts as they arrived on camels too numerous to count. They remained until the land was stripped bare, and Israel was reduced to starvation. Once again, our people cried out to the Lord for help.

It is written that the angel of the Lord was sent to sit beneath the great tree at Ophrah, which belonged to Joash of the clan of Abiezer and the tribe of Manasseh. Gideon, Joash's son, was threshing wheat at the bottom of a winepress to hide grain from the Midianites when the angel said to him, *"Mighty hero, the Lord is with you!"* [2]

"Sir," Gideon replied, *"if the Lord is with us, why has all this happened to us? And where are all the miracles our ancestors told us about? Didn't they say,*

'The Lord brought us up out of Egypt'? But now the Lord has abandoned us and handed us over to the Midianites."[3]

The angel of the Lord turned to him and said, "I am sending you! Go with the strength you have, and rescue Israel from the Midianites."[4]

"But Lord," Gideon replied, "how can I rescue Israel? My clan is the weakest in the whole tribe of Manasseh, and I am the least in my entire family!"[5]

The Lord said to him, "I will be with you. And you will destroy the Midianites as if you were fighting against one man."[6]

Gideon responded, "If You are truly going to use me to rescue Israel as You promised, prove it to me in this way. I will put a wool fleece on the threshing floor tonight. If the fleece is wet with dew in the morning but the ground is dry, then I will know that You are going to help me rescue Israel as you promised."[7]

When Gideon got up early the next morning the ground was dry, but when he squeezed the fleece, he wrung out a bowlful of water.

"Lord, please don't be angry with me," Gideon said, "but let me make one more request. Let me use the fleece for one more test. This time let the fleece remain dry while the ground around it is wet with dew."[8]

That night God again did as Gideon asked. The fleece was dry in the morning, but the ground was covered with dew.

You may have heard how Gideon then sent messengers throughout Manasseh, Asher, Zebulun, and Naphtali, including our city of Kedesh. My grandfather Shimea responded to the call and joined the 32,000 men who gathered at the spring of Harod to fight the Midianites.

My grandfather often told me the story of what happened next, and I hung on his every word. More often than not, those conversations went something like this.

"*The Lord told Gideon, 'You have too many warriors with you. If I let all of you fight the Midianites, the Israelites will boast to me that they saved themselves by their own strength. Therefore, tell the people, "Whoever is timid or afraid may leave this mountain and go home."'*"[9]

"Twenty-two thousand of them went home," my grandfather continued, "leaving only 10,000 of us who were willing to fight. But the Lord told Gideon, '*There are still too many! Bring them down to the spring, and I will test them to determine who will go with you and who will not.*'"[10]

"When Gideon took us down to the water, the Lord told him, '*Divide the men into two groups. In one group put all those who cup water in their hands and lap it up with their tongues like dogs. In the other group put all those who kneel down and drink with their mouths in the stream.*'"[11]

"Only 300 of us drank from our hands. All the others got down on their knees and drank with their mouths in the stream.

"The Lord then told Gideon, '*With these 300 men I will rescue you and give you victory over the Midianites. Send all the others home.*'"[12]

My grandfather's voice softened. "It seemed impossible. Just 300 of us to face that massive Midianite horde? Every breath was a prayer to the Lord."

With each telling of the story, I would lean forward, chin resting upon my grandfather's knee, and ask the same questions. "Grandfather, what was going through your mind? How did you feel when so many left, and only a few of you remained?"

My grandfather looked down at me, his face stern yet kind. "We were fearful, Asaph, but it was a fear balanced with faith. The Lord had chosen us, and it was both humbling and daunting. Many of us wondered if Gideon was truly hearing from the Lord, but deep down, we knew God was at work."

He gave a faint smile. "Gideon was steady, though. Not once did he doubt in front of us."

Another voice spoke up from across the room. My cousin Ahio always had a hundred questions. "But Grandfather, what kind of strategy could 300 men possibly have against so many? It's like a shepherd trying to fend off a pack of wolves."

My grandfather chuckled. "The Lord's strategy, Ahio! Gideon gathered us around that night and told us each to take a trumpet, a torch, and a clay jar." His eyes sparkled as he recounted the scene. "Imagine us— warriors armed with nothing but noise and light! We looked at each other, wondering if he'd finally lost his mind. But Gideon's faith didn't waver."

I could picture the scene—300 men, tired and anxious, clutching their unconventional weapons as the stars stretched out above them. It must have seemed almost foolish, yet awe-inspiring, to trust that such a plan would be successful.

So I had to ask the question. "But did you believe it would work?"

My grandfather slowly nodded. "Yes, I did. I had seen God's hand too many times to doubt His power, even if His methods weren't what we expected."

He looked around the circle of his grandchildren, his voice carrying a deep reverence. "That night, as we stood around the enemy camp, torches hidden under jars and trumpets silent, I knew the Lord was present. The silence was thick, almost alive."

He straightened, reliving the moment. "When Gideon gave the signal, we smashed the jars, raised the torches high, and blasted the trumpets. We shouted, 'For the Lord and for Gideon!' The noise must have sounded like a thunderstorm in that valley, echoing off the mountains. The Midianites awoke in terror, stumbling over each other in their confusion."

I could barely contain my excitement. "And then what happened?"

"They turned on one another," my grandfather continued, his voice shaking. "The Lord sent such panic among them they believed we were a vast army surrounding them. They slashed their own allies, retreating in chaos. We watched as they scattered and fled."

"God truly fought for Israel that night," my father added quietly. He hadn't spoken much, but I saw the same pride and faith shining in his eyes. "He proved that with Him, numbers mean nothing."

One of my younger cousins asked, "What happened after that?"

My grandfather placed a hand on the boy's shoulder. "That victory broke the Midianite oppression. They fled, and we pursued them until their power over Israel was completely shattered. From that day, there was peace in the land once more."

The fire crackled as we sat in thoughtful silence, pondering our ancestors' history and faith. I knew these stories by heart, but tonight they felt even more vivid, woven with courage and an unwavering trust in Jehovah.

After a pause, my grandfather looked at us with a glint in his eye. "But remember this, my sons. It's not the number of men that wins a battle, nor the strength of arms alone, but obedience to the Lord's call. Our fathers knew this truth, and we must remember it too."

I nodded, a lump forming in my throat. The Lord had fought for Israel before, and I felt He would do so again. This was the faith of our forefathers, and it would be the foundation for us as well.

As the fire dwindled, my father rose, wrapping his shawl around him. "Come, let's sleep. The Lord gave us these stories for a reason, and perhaps we'll find out why soon enough."

He looked at me with a knowing smile. "Asaph, you're starting to see what our forefathers have passed down to us. Don't forget these lessons."

I bowed my head, taking in his words.

~

3

"GIVE US A KING!"

~

*F*ollowing Gideon's forty-year rule, and despite the bravery of judges like Samson, Tola, and Jair, the people of Israel continued to subject themselves to pagan rule in disobedience to God. My father, Berechiah, was two years old on that fateful day when the Philistines captured the Ark of God.

Seven months later, after the Ark returned to its temporary resting place at Kiriath-jearim, the prophet Samuel summoned the Israelites, saying, *"If you want to return to the Lord with all your hearts, then get rid of your foreign gods and your images of Ashtoreth. Turn your hearts to the Lord and obey Him alone; then He will rescue you from the Philistines."*[1]

The Israelites disposed of their images of Baal and Ashtoreth and bowed their hearts in worship of the Lord. Samuel gathered them at Mizpah and, in a great ceremony, drew water from a well and poured it out before the Lord. The people fasted all day and together confessed they had sinned against the Lord.

When the Philistine rulers heard that Israel had gathered at Mizpah, and Samuel was now their judge, they mobilized their army and advanced. The approaching enemy frightened the Israelites. *"Don't stop pleading with the Lord our God to save us from the Philistines!"*[2] they begged Samuel.

So Samuel presented the Lord with a young lamb as a burnt offering. He pleaded with the Lord to help Israel, and the Lord answered him. Just as Samuel was sacrificing the lamb, the Philistines arrived to attack Israel. But the Lord spoke with a mighty voice of thunder from heaven, and the Philistines were thrown into such confusion that the Israelites defeated them. The men of Israel chased them from Mizpah, slaughtering them along the way.

As a reminder of what God had done on behalf of His people, Samuel took a large stone and placed it along that path. He named it Ebenezer, which means "the stone of help," for he said, *"Up to this point the Lord has helped us!"*[3]

The Philistines were resoundingly defeated and did not invade Israel again for some time. The Israelite villages near Ekron and Gath, previously captured by the Philistines, were restored to Israel, along with the rest of the territory that had been taken.

Samuel continued as Israel's judge into his old age, at which time he appointed his two oldest sons to take his place. But sadly, they were not like their father. They were greedy, accepting bribes, and perverting justice for their personal advantage. As a result, the leaders of Israel confronted Samuel saying, *"You are now old, and your sons are not like you. Give us a king like all the nations have."*[4]

When Samuel took their request before the Lord, He replied, *"Do everything they say to you, for they are rejecting Me, not you. They don't want Me to be their king any longer. Ever since I brought them from Egypt, they have continually abandoned Me and followed other gods. And now they are giving you the same treatment. Do as they ask, but solemnly warn them about the way a king will reign over them."* [(5)]

So Samuel passed on the Lord's warning to the people. *"This is how a king will reign over you,"* he said. *"The king will draft your sons and assign them to his chariots and his charioteers, making them run before his chariots. Some will be generals and captains in his army, some will be forced to plow in his fields and harvest his crops, and some will make his weapons and chariot equipment. The king will take your daughters from you and force them to cook and bake and make perfumes for him. He will take away the best of your fields and vineyards and olive groves and give them to his own officials. He will take a tenth of your grain and your grape harvest and distribute it among his officers and attendants. He will take your male and female slaves and demand the finest of your cattle and donkeys for his own use. He will demand a tenth of your flocks, and you will be his slaves. When that day comes, you will beg for relief from this king you are demanding, but then the Lord will not help you."* [(6)]

But the people ignored God's warning and demanded a king.

As my father and I walked back home, we discussed the stories told that evening. "Our people wanted a king," my father said, his voice full of regret. "They wanted to be like other nations. They saw the power, the grandeur of foreign kings, and believed that such a leader would give us security. But they forgot—it was Jehovah who led us, not any man."

My father shook his head, brows knitted in frustration. "And after every-thing God had done for them! He delivered us time and again—by His hand alone. Yet our people could not see it. They wanted a human king they could see and touch, not the unseen God who had faithfully guided us from Egypt."

I could not imagine why our ancestors had reacted this way. "But Father, didn't they understand the warning Samuel gave them? Surely, they heard the burden a king would bring."

Father sighed deeply. "Samuel's words were clear, Asaph, yet their hearts were stubborn. He warned them how a king would conscript their sons, seize their fields, and tax their harvests. He warned that they would become slaves to this king. But even then, they refused to listen." He paused, his gaze intense. "They wanted the strength and security they saw in the armies of other kingdoms, not the strength that comes from trusting the Almighty."

"So why did God let them have a king if He knew it would lead to hardship?" I asked.

"Because our Lord is not one to force devotion," my father replied in a firm voice. "He allows us to make our own choices, even when they lead to pain. He allows us to learn through the consequences of our own decisions. God knew that Israel's demand for a king was a rejection of His own kingship. Yet, in His patience, He allowed it. He gave them Saul, a king who looked the part—tall, strong, handsome. And for a time, he led well until his heart turned proud, and he strayed from God."

I looked up at my father, captivated by his words. "So even when God gives us what we want, there are still lessons to be learned?"

"Exactly," Father replied, his expression softening. "Israel wanted to be like other nations, but they were not like any other nation—they were chosen, set apart to be a light in the darkness. Yet they could not see this. And so, the kings who followed would teach us both the glories and the pains of earthly rule."

∾

4

A KING IS ANOINTED

~

*A*ccording to the chronicles of our people, there was a man of wealth and influence from the tribe of Benjamin named Kish. He was the son of Abiel and grandson of Zeror, from the family of Becorath and the clan of Aphiah. Kish's son Saul was considered the most handsome man in all of Israel—standing head and shoulders above anyone else in the land.

One day, Kish directed Saul to find a coffle of donkeys that had strayed. Saul, along with one of his family's servants, traveled throughout the hill country of Ephraim in search of the animals. Saul was about to return home empty-handed when his servant said, *"I've just thought of something! There is a man of God who lives in Gilgal. He is held in high honor by all the people because everything he says comes true. Let's go find him. Perhaps he can tell us which way to go."* [1]

"But we don't have anything to offer him," Saul replied. *"Even our food is gone."* [2]

"*Well,*" the servant continued, "*I have one small silver piece. We can at least offer it to him and see what happens.*"[3]

So the two began their journey into town to find the prophet. Along the way, they met several young women coming to the edge of town to draw water.

"*Is the prophet here today?*"[4] Saul asked the women.

"Yes," they replied. "*Stay right on this road. He has just arrived at the town gates to take part in a public sacrifice up on the hill. If you hurry, you can catch up with him before he goes up the hill to eat. The guests won't start until he arrives to bless the food.*"[5]

Also written in our annals is that the previous day the Lord told the prophet Samuel, "*About this time tomorrow I will send you a man from the land of Benjamin. Anoint him to be leader of My people, Israel. He will rescue them from the Philistines, for I have looked down on My people in mercy and have heard their cry.*"[6]

As Samuel saw Saul approaching, the Lord told him, "*That's the man I told you about! He will rule My people.*"[7]

When Saul reached the gates, he asked Samuel, "*Can you please tell me where the prophet's house is?*"[8]

"*I am he!*" Samuel replied. "*Go on up the hill ahead of me to the place of sacrifice, and we'll eat together. In the morning I will tell you what you want to know and send you on your way. And don't worry about those donkeys that were lost three days ago, for they have been found. And I am here to tell you that you and your family are the focus of all Israel's hopes.*"[9]

"*But I'm only from Benjamin,*" Saul responded. "*It is the smallest tribe in Israel, and my family is one of the least important of all the families of that tribe! Why are you talking like this to me?*"[10]

Saul was mystified when Samuel led him to the banquet and placed him and his servant at the head of the table, honoring them above the other guests. The finest piece of meat was set before Saul as the guest of honor.

After the feast, Samuel took Saul to the roof and prepared him a bed. The next morning, Samuel walked with Saul and his servant to the edge of town. He then told Saul to send his servant on ahead.

"*Stay here,*" Samuel advised Saul, "*for I have received a special message for you from God.*"[11]

Samuel then took a flask of olive oil and poured it over Saul's head. He kissed Saul and said, "*I am doing this because the Lord has appointed you to be the ruler over Israel, His special possession. When you leave me today, you will see two men beside Rachel's tomb at Zelzah, on the border of Benjamin. They will tell you that the donkeys have been found and that your father has stopped worrying about them and is now worried about you. He is asking, 'Have you seen my son?'*

"*When you get to the oak of Tabor, you will see three men coming toward you who are on their way to worship God at Bethel. One will be bringing three young goats, another will have three loaves of bread, and the third will be carrying a wineskin full of wine. They will greet you and offer you two of the loaves, which you are to accept.*

"*When you arrive at Gibeah of God, where the garrison of the Philistines is located, you will meet a band of prophets coming down from the place of worship. They will be playing a harp, a tambourine, a flute, and a lyre, and they will be prophesying. At that time, the Spirit of the Lord will come powerfully upon you, and you will prophesy with them. You will be changed into a different person.*

"After these signs take place, do what must be done, for God is with you. Then go down to Gilgal ahead of me. I will join you there to sacrifice burnt offerings and peace offerings. You must wait for seven days until I arrive and give you further instructions." (12)

It is written that as Saul turned to leave, God gave him a new heart, and all Samuel's signs were fulfilled that day. When Saul and his servant arrived at Gibeah, they saw a group of prophets coming toward them. Then the Spirit of God came powerfully upon Saul, and he, too, began to prophesy.

When those who knew Saul heard about it, they exclaimed, *"What? Is even Saul a prophet? How did the son of Kish become a prophet?"* (13)

And one of those standing nearby said, *"Can anyone become a prophet, no matter who his father is?"* (14)

Seven days later, when Samuel arrived at Gilgal, he called all the people of Israel to meet before the Lord at Mizpah so he could address them.

"This is what the Lord, the God of Israel, has declared: I brought you from Egypt and rescued you from the Egyptians and from all of the nations that were oppressing you. But though I have rescued you from your misery and distress, you have rejected your God today and have said, 'No, we want a king instead!' Now, therefore, present yourselves before the Lord by tribes and clans." (15)

Samuel brought all the tribes of Israel before the Lord, and the tribe of Benjamin was chosen by lot. Then he brought each family of the tribe of Benjamin before the Lord, and the family of the Matrites was chosen. And finally Saul, son of Kish, was chosen from among them. But when they looked for him, he had disappeared! So they asked the Lord, *"Where is he?"* (16)

And the Lord replied, *"He is hiding among the luggage."*[17]

So they found him and brought him out, and he towered above everyone else. Then Samuel told the people, *"This is the man the Lord has chosen as your king. No one in all Israel is like him!"*[18]

And all the people shouted, *"Long live the king!"*[19]

One month later, Saul led 300,000 men of Israel and 30,000 of Judah to defeat King Nahash of Ammon who had threatened the Israelite city of Jabesh-gilead. Following the resounding victory, leaders from all of Israel returned to Gilgal. In a solemn ceremony before the Lord, they crowned Saul their king. And all the people rejoiced.

In the tenth year of King Saul's rule, three mothers each gave birth to a baby boy. Unbeknownst to their families, the three lives would be inextricably linked as the boys grew into manhood. The first boy born was I— Asaph, son of Berechiah of the tribe of Levi. The second was Nathan of the tribe of Ephraim, who would become a student of the prophet Samuel. The youngest boy was David, son of Jesse of the tribe of Judah—a shepherd who would one day become king.

Though we came from different tribes and different backgrounds, the Lord God Jehovah would order our steps to become a three-strand cord.

∾

5

THE UNCHALLENGED GIANT

~

*T*his may sound far-fetched, but I truly believe my first memories of my mother, Rachel, were while I was still in her womb. I can remember her angelic voice as she lifted up loving praises to Jehovah God. I have always believed the angels quieted their singing when they heard her melodious worship so her voice might be heard filling all of heaven.

However, when I was three years old, my mother died while giving birth to my brother, Zechariah. Our father often told us that Jehovah God brought her into His presence so she might lead the celestial host in praising Him. "You will never be closer to your mother than when you are praising the Lord," my father would say. "Listen for her voice, and you will hear it."

As Levites, as well as sons of a musical family, my brother and I were trained from an early age to be as proficient as our father on a variety of musical instruments. We learned to play the lyre, the cymbals, the harp, and the trumpet. But there was no denying that I alone had inherited our mother's gift of singing. Zechariah would follow in the ways of our father and be content to make a joyful noise.

We were members of the ancestral family of Gershon, Levi's eldest son, and our duties related to the house of the Lord were established by Moses when the tabernacle was first completed in the wilderness. Our responsibilities included erecting, dismantling, and transporting the curtains, outer coverings, courtyard walls, and entrances of the tabernacle. As you can imagine, those duties were exhausting throughout the years as our people wandered in the wilderness.

After the conquest and division of the Promised Land, Joshua led our people to erect the Tabernacle in the city of Shiloh in the land of Ephraim. It remained there for slightly less than 400 years. Though the tabernacle never moved during that time, nine generations of my family lived in readiness for just such an occasion. All the men between the ages of thirty and fifty were trained, practiced, and prepared in case the command was given.

Beginning when we were children, Zechariah and I were trained in music, poetry, and the teachings of Moses. We learned how to worship Jehovah God, the Giver of all things, as we worked around our home and in the field cultivating our garden's produce.

"Brother, what is that tune you are humming?" Zechariah asked one day as we harvested the crops. "I have never heard it before."

"I don't really know," I laughed. "It is a melody that continues to repeat itself in my head."

"Well, it is a beautiful tune," my brother commented.

"Perhaps I should write a poem to accompany the melody as a praise to our Lord," I replied, more to myself than to Zechariah.

When I was fourteen, the Lord came to me in a vision. I was standing on a hill overlooking a field where a shepherd boy, about my age, was grazing his sheep. His rugged appearance was topped by a wild mop of curls, and his eyes were bright and alert reflecting wisdom beyond his years.

Clad in the simple garments of a shepherd, the boy's demeanor exuded a quiet confidence. His countenance reflected a gentleness that comforted his sheep and a calm assurance they were safe.

Though I saw no one else with him, a voice called out to me, "See this one of humble appearance. I have given him a heart like mine, and I will make him king over the people who are called by My name."

"But, Lord, we already have a king, and his name is Saul."

The Lord replied, *"I am sorry that I ever made Saul king, for he has not been loyal to Me and has disobeyed Me."*[1]

Suddenly, a lion charged from nearby brush and, in one fluid movement, captured a lamb in his jaws. But before the lion could retreat with its prey, the shepherd used his club to strike the beast in the center of its forehead. The lion's jaw sprung open, and the lamb fell to its feet, scurrying away to safety.

The voice again addressed me. "Asaph, I have chosen you to serve this king all of his days. Protect and support him in his journey to the throne, and help him lead My people in their journey before My throne. In so doing, you will be honoring and serving Me."

As I continued to watch the shepherd, I knew I had been given a divine charge to be a part of God's unfolding plan. I had no idea who the shepherd boy was, but I knew God would show me in His time—and I would need to serve him from that moment forward. When I awoke, I was back in my own bed. The shepherd, his sheep, and the field were gone, but I knew my mandate from the Lord was not.

As the months passed, the ongoing skirmishes between the Philistines and Israelites continued. The Philistines controlled the coastal regions of the land of Canaan, but they also wanted control of the central hill country and fertile agricultural valleys inhabited by the Israelites. Throughout the reign of King Saul, the Philistines were a constant threat to Israel and posed a significant military challenge to Israel's sovereignty.

The Philistines also tried to intimidate my people. Those efforts came to a climax when a giant warrior named Goliath arrived from Gath. The Philistine army gathered in the Valley of Elah with their giant champion who boastfully taunted the Israelite army. He was over nine feet tall, wearing a bronze helmet and a coat of armor weighing 125 pounds.

He also wore bronze leggings and slung a javelin over his back. The shaft of his spear was as heavy and as thick as a weaver's beam, tipped with an iron spearhead that weighed fifteen pounds. An armor bearer walked ahead of him carrying a massive shield.

The day Goliath arrived, he stood on the front line of the Philistine side of the valley and shouted to the Israelites, *"Do you need a whole army to settle this? Choose someone to fight for you, and I will represent the Philistines. We will settle this dispute in single combat! If your man is able to kill me, then we will be your slaves. However, if I kill him, you will be our slaves! I defy the armies of Israel! Send me a man who will fight with me!"*[2]

Word quickly spread throughout Israel about this giant who was terrorizing King Saul and his warriors. Men from far and wide journeyed to the Valley of Elah—including Zechariah and me. Though as Levites we were prevented from fighting, we weren't without curiosity. We wanted to see this mighty warrior!

We could not believe our eyes. No one in all of Israel could compare to Goliath's size or might. No volunteers accepted his challenge for fear the battle would be over before it began, and our people would be enslaved by the Philistines. I would like to tell you our people began to pray and seek God. But the reality is, we were blinded by fear.

For forty days, morning and evening, the giant strutted among us repeating his challenge. Word began to spread that King Saul had offered a reward: the hand of one of his daughters in marriage and exemption of taxes to the man who killed the giant.

However, the Israelite men just shook their heads and responded, "The only catch is you must live to receive your reward!" No one stepped forward ... until one day.

～

6

A DAY I WILL NEVER FORGET

~

*T*he sun was beginning to sink in the Valley of Elah, casting long shadows across the dry, rocky terrain. The Israelite and Philistine forces were lined up facing each other at 1,000 paces. This had been their practice twice a day for forty days. An obvious unease emanated from every man gathered. Soon, the giant emerged from the Philistine ranks to again taunt the army of Israel.

Zechariah and I were standing in the midst of the crowd watching the spectacle. My heart was pounding when I suddenly noticed one of the Israelite warriors withdrawing from the battle lines. He was confronting another who appeared to be about my age and who was dressed like a shepherd. The youth looked familiar to me.

"What are you doing here, David?" the older warrior shouted at the shepherd. "Why aren't you tending the sheep like you are supposed to be doing? Did our father give you the day off, or have you slipped away to spy on the men here defending our nation's honor?"

"It doesn't appear anyone is defending our nation's honor, Eliab!" the boy called David retorted. *"Who is this pagan Philistine anyway that he is allowed to defy the armies of the living God? What will a man get for killing him and putting an end to his abuse of Israel?"* [1]

"Is your arrogance so great that you think you can defeat this giant?" Eliab taunted.

"What have I done now?" David replied. *"I was only asking a question.*[2] But yes, if no one else will go and fight him, I will!"

By now the brothers' shouting had drawn the attention of everyone standing nearby.

"Don't be ridiculous!" Eliab snorted.

But David persisted. *"I have been taking care of my father's sheep. When a lion or a bear comes to steal a lamb from the flock, I go after it with a club and take the lamb from its mouth. If the animal turns on me, I catch it by the jaw and club it to death. I have done this to both lions and bears, and I'll do it to this pagan Philistine, too, for he has defied the armies of the living God!"* [3]

I quickly realized where I had seen this shepherd before; he was the boy in my vision from the Lord! If he was the one God had chosen to make king, I knew he was no ordinary man. And I was confident God would enable him to defeat this giant.

"The Lord who saved me from the claws of the lion and the bear will save me from this Philistine!" [4] David continued.

Just then, King Saul appeared and the crowd parted so he could see the shepherd. As he looked at David, he said, "But you are little more than a boy, and this giant has been in the army since before you were born!"

"Yes, my king," David said with his head bowed, "but the living God will grant me victory over him."

After a few moments of silence, the king consented. *"All right, go ahead,"* he said. *"And may the Lord be with you!"*[(5)]

The king instructed his servants to bring his own armor to put on David—a bronze helmet and a coat of overlapping metal plates called mail. But when David strapped it on and tried to walk a few steps, he started to protest.

"I cannot wear these! They are too big for me, and I'm not used to them. They will hinder me more than protect me."

After removing the armor, he walked over to a nearby stream and picked up five smooth stones, carefully placing them in his shepherd's bag. Then, armed only with his shepherd's staff and sling, he walked across the field to confront the giant.

Once Goliath realized David's intention was to confront him, he sneered in contempt.

"Am I a dog," he roared, *"that you come at me with a stick? Come toward me, and I will give your flesh to the birds and wild animals!"*[(6)]

But David did not flinch. He stood his ground, his voice clear and strong as he responded.

"You come to me with sword, spear, and javelin, but I come to you in the name of the Lord Almighty—the God of the armies of Israel, whom you have defied. Today He will conquer you, and I will kill you, cutting off your head. And then I will give the dead bodies of your men to the birds and the wild animals, and the whole world will know that there is a God in Israel. And everyone will know that the Lord does not need weapons to rescue His people. It is His battle, not ours, and He will give you to us!"(7)

I felt a chill run down my spine at David's words. They were so powerful the air seemed to crackle with anticipation. I found myself gripping the hilt of the sword hanging around my waist—not out of fear but out of an overwhelming sense of awe. This was not just a battle between two men; this was a battle between the forces of heaven and earth.

As the giant moved closer to attack, David swiftly ran to meet him. Reaching into his shepherd's pouch, he took out a stone and hurled it from his sling, hitting the Philistine in the only unprotected part of his forehead.

We heard a sickening thud as the stone sank into the giant's skull, and for a moment, time seemed to stand still. Goliath's eyes widened in shock, his body swaying as if he couldn't quite believe what was happening. Then, with a thunderous crash, the giant toppled forward, hitting the ground with a force that shook the earth.

A stunned silence fell over the valley. The Philistines stared in disbelief at their fallen champion, and so did I. Goliath, the terror of Israel, was dead, slain by a single stone from the hand of a shepherd boy.

"Brother, are my eyes deceiving me, or did you just witness the same thing I did?" Zechariah asked, gazing up at me.

"Yes," I responded, looking on in shock. "A shepherd boy just felled the giant with a small rock! If I had not been here to see it for myself, I would not have believed it."

"Surely, he must be a man of Almighty God," Zechariah said, his voice filled with amazement.

David did not hesitate to finish his job. He ran forward, drew Goliath's own sword, and cut off the giant's head, holding it aloft for all to see.

When the Philistines realized their champion was dead, they turned and ran—pursued by an equally surprised, though triumphant, Israelite force. I couldn't help but smile when I saw Eliab hurry over to his brother and honor David by bowing as one warrior to another. But I caught a glimpse of David's heart and soul when he gave his brother a loving embrace. Whatever words had been exchanged earlier were now forgiven and forgotten.

After Eliab joined the other Israelites in pursuit of the Philistines, I approached David to congratulate him on his victory. I introduced myself and told him about the vision from God.

"David, that day I pledged to serve, support, and protect you in your journey to the throne," I said, "and to help you lead God's people in rightly worshiping Him. Since He has now brought us together, my service to you begins today. I am forever your servant."

"Well, in that case, Asaph," David replied with a slight grin, "help me carry this Philistine giant's armor!"

As we made our way across the field—David carrying the giant's head and sword, me carrying the giant's helmet and armor—we were intercepted by Abner, King Saul's general.

"David," he called out, "the king summons you to his tent so he can extend his gratitude for your act of bravery." He then turned toward me and asked, "And who are you?"

Before I could answer, David replied, "His name is Asaph and he is a Levite, a servant of God, and one who has become my trusted companion. I go nowhere without him by my side. Surely the king will welcome him as well. Besides, as you can see, he helps me carry some weighty trophies I am certain the king will want to examine."

"Of course he can join us," Abner responded. "I am certain the king will receive him if he is by your side."

As we followed Abner, David and I turned to each other and exchanged impish grins. I knew I would go with David wherever the Lord led him. And in my heart, I again vowed to use my gifts to glorify the God of Israel who had just delivered us all from the hand of our enemies.

When we reached the king's tent, Abner had us wait outside so he could announce David's arrival. I grew unsettled when I heard the king raise his voice in displeasure. I wondered if he were bothered by my being there. Apparently, his servants calmed him, and I heard him say, "All right then, see them both in!"

～

7

THE ROAD TO THE CROWN

～

*L*ife took on a new rhythm after David defeated Goliath. At first, the shepherd boy returned to Bethlehem to tend his father's sheep. His absence gave me time to consider how his faith had struck me to the core. It wasn't just the victory over Goliath that had moved me—it was David's certainty in the Lord, his unyielding belief that God would deliver Israel. I felt something awaken in me that day, a sense of calling beyond my musical talent.

Unfortunately, the years that followed were filled with tension and change. I had glimpsed the beginning of David's rise that day in the Valley of Elah, but now he was on a slow and uncertain path that led from the battlefield to the throne of Israel. I watched from the sidelines as my friend, the shepherd-turned-hero, found himself both celebrated and hunted, moving from the pasture to the palace and then to the wilderness, as King Saul's jealousy turned murderous.

What took place at the Valley of Elah had become something of a legend throughout Israel and Judah. People were in awe of the boy who had faced the giant with nothing but a sling and the name of the Lord. But while the songs and stories about David grew, so did the darkness surrounding him. King Saul, once a towering figure of leadership, had become extremely paranoid. His eyes, once kind, were now clouded with suspicion, especially toward David, whose fame only seemed to increase.

Though he and I were both still young, we began to understand the shifting currents of power and fear that moved through the court of Israel —David as the one who was clearly appearing to be God's anointed and me as a close observer.

My father, brother, and I continued to serve as musicians before the Ark, somewhat isolated from the events at Gibeah, where Saul reigned. However, it wasn't long before David's situation began to directly affect us.

It started gradually. First, David stopped appearing regularly at court, and rumors began circulating about Saul's increasingly erratic behavior. Then, one evening as I sat composing a melody, a messenger arrived breathless, urgently asking for my father.

"Asaph," my father said after a hurried conversation with the man. "Pack your things. We're going to Gibeah. It seems the king has requested the Levites for special service there."

I hadn't heard of any major feast or festival that required the presence of my family. But there was something in my father's voice—something tense —that made me keep my questions to myself.

The journey to Gibeah was uneventful, but the air seemed heavier as we drew closer. We arrived to find the palace in a state of disarray. Soldiers moved about uneasily, and courtiers spoke in hushed tones. I followed my father through the hallways, my concern growing with every step. It wasn't until we reached a dimly lit chamber near the king's quarters that I saw him—David, his face grim but composed, seated with a lyre in his lap.

"Asaph," David said, rising to embrace me as if no time had passed. "I'm glad you've come."

"What's happening?" I asked quietly. "Why is everyone so … on edge?"

David's face tightened, and his eyes flitted around the room before he spoke.

"King Saul is no longer the man he was. His spirit is tormented, and he sees enemies in every shadow. I've been playing the harp, hoping it would soothe him, but he's growing worse. He tried to kill me."

My breath caught in my throat. "Kill you? But why? You've done nothing but serve him faithfully!"

David shook his head. "It's not about what I've done. He fears the Lord's favor is no longer with him, and that it rests with me. His jealousy—it's consuming him."

Before I could respond, there was a commotion in the hallway. The door burst open, and the king strode in, his eyes wild and his movements erratic. I had seen the king only a few times since the day David defeated the giant, but it was always from a distance during grand ceremonies. This man before me, with disheveled hair and loose-fitting robes, was a shadow of the powerful king he had once been.

"David!" Saul bellowed, his voice hoarse with rage. "You think you can hide from me? I know what you're doing, conspiring behind my back, plotting to take my throne!"

David stood his ground, his voice calm. "My lord, I serve you and you alone. I have done nothing but honor you and the Lord."

"Lies!" Saul spat, his hand twitching toward the spear at his side.

I froze, my heart pounding, as I saw the king's fingers wrap around the weapon.

David's hand moved slowly to his lyre. "Let me play for you, my lord. Let the music soothe your spirit as it has before."

For a moment, it seemed the king might refuse, but then he slumped into a nearby chair, waving his hand dismissively.

"Play, then. But know this, David—your time is coming. I will not be undone by a shepherd boy."

David began to play, his fingers moving over the strings with practiced ease, a soft, mournful melody filling the room. I watched Saul's face slowly relax, his tension easing as the sound washed over him. The music seemed to push back the darkness, if only for a moment.

But I knew this peace was temporary. When the song ended, Saul rose abruptly and left without a word, his shadow trailing after him like a storm cloud.

David set his lyre down with a sigh, running a hand through his hair. "This situation is becoming wretched," he said softly. "I don't know how much longer I can stay here."

"What will you do?" I asked.

David looked up at me, his eyes weary but determined. "I must leave, and soon. The Lord has a plan, though I don't fully understand it yet. But one thing I know for certain. I cannot stay here and wait for Saul to kill me."

The thought of David fleeing, hunted like a criminal, weighed heavily on my heart. The people of Israel loved David. Everyone had heard the songs the women sang: *"Saul has slain his thousands, and David his tens of thousands."*[(1)] But the people's adoration only fueled Saul's hatred.

For the next few months, David disappeared. News of him trickled in sporadically—stories of him hiding in caves, evading Saul's men, gathering a group of loyal followers who believed, as I did, that David was the rightful king chosen by God. My family and I maintained our duty of leading worship in Gibeah, but my heart was with my friend. I prayed constantly for David's safety, pouring my fears and hopes for the future into my music.

After years of waiting, we received the news that changed everything.

Saul was dead.

The battle against the Philistines had taken place on Mount Gilboa. Saul, gravely wounded, had fallen on his sword rather than be captured by the enemy. His sons, including Jonathan, had been slain alongside him. The king was gone, and with him, the reign of his family.

David was now the anointed king of Judah, and soon, all of Israel. I rejoiced by writing this psalm: *"He chose his servant David, calling him from the sheep pens. He took David from tending the ewes and lambs and made him the shepherd of Jacob's descendants—God's own people, Israel."*[(2)]

David led his troops to Jerusalem to defeat the Jebusites and conquer their stronghold. He had selected Jerusalem to be the seat of his rule—and it was there that the Ark of God would be placed. Our family was one of the first to make the move from Gibeah to Jerusalem.

The faint strains of a lyre drifted through the open window of our new house, carried on the cool evening breeze. Inside, I sat cross-legged on the floor, my fingers deftly plucking the strings of my instrument. The notes filled the room with a peaceful melody, echoing the joy that had now settled in my heart.

My father sat nearby, sharpening a blade. Though he was no longer a soldier, old habits die hard. He would now serve as the Doorkeeper of the Ark of God. The Ark was soon to be brought to Jerusalem under King David's command, and my father had been appointed to protect it—a role that filled him with great pride and solemn responsibility.

The door to the house creaked open, and I glanced up to see my brother wearing a bright smile. Zechariah had been at the tabernacle in Gibeon earlier that day, assisting in the worship service there. He was always full of energy, a young man who thrived in his duties as a Levite.

"Asaph!" Zechariah's voice boomed as he crossed the room, his arms open wide. "You've been practicing, I can tell! The music's flowing through these walls like a river."

I grinned, setting down my lyre. "I've been working on a new melody. I want it ready by the time King David returns to lead us in bringing the Ark of God from the home of Abinadab back here to Jerusalem."

～

8

A DAY THAT BEGAN IN JOY

$\sim$

*W*hen David returned to Jerusalem, I was one of the first to greet him. The young man I had known, the shepherd boy who had slain Goliath, had been transformed. David now carried himself with the weight of kingship, his eyes wiser, his face more weathered by the trials he had endured. But when he saw me, his expression softened, and the old warmth returned.

"Asaph," David said, clasping my arm. "It has been too long."

I smiled, my heart swelling with joy. "It is good to see you again, my king."

David chuckled, shaking his head. "Don't call me that. Not when it's just the two of us."

I laughed. "Fine, but don't expect the same from everyone else. The people are already singing new songs about you."

David's expression grew serious. "Songs and titles mean little, Asaph. I am king now, yes, but I remember the fields of Bethlehem. I know whom I serve."

And it was true. Despite the crown on his head, David's heart remained firmly rooted in his faith. He had not forgotten the Lord who had delivered him from the hand of Saul and every other danger he faced. That night, David and I sat together under the stars, sharing stories of the years past.

"Asaph, I had to hide out in caves and in the wilderness to stay a step ahead of Saul's men. But through it all, the Lord sustained me. Even when hope seemed distant, I prayed and wrote psalms asking God for protection and praising Him for his unfailing love."

David went on to tell me about the men who had faithfully followed him even when there was no clear path to the throne. And I, in turn, talked about the music I had composed to play in the tabernacle, and how the Lord's presence had filled the people with peace.

As the night wore on, we began to speak of the future.

"I want you to lead the music before the Ark," David said softly. "But more than that, I want you to help me write new songs—songs that will remind the people of who our God is. Songs that will be sung not just in the courts of kings but in the hearts of all who follow the Lord."

My heart leaped at the thought. To compose alongside David, to bring the words of the king into melodies that would echo through the generations —it was a calling I had never dared dream. But now, standing at the threshold of a new era, I knew this was the path the Lord had prepared for me.

"I would be honored," I replied.

And so, our friendship deepened—not just as companions but as servants of the Lord, united in purpose. Together, we would write the songs of Israel, songs that would tell of the mighty deeds of God, of His mercy, and of His faithfulness.

The next morning dawned bright and full of expectation. For years, the Ark of God, the holiest object in our history, had been resting in the house of Abinadab in Kiriath-Jearim. David, now king over all of Israel, had declared it was time to bring the Ark to Jerusalem, the city that would be the center of worship for the nation—and today was the day.

Standing alongside my father and brother as we waited to assemble, I felt a rush of excitement.

"It's finally happening," Zechariah said, fiddling with the strap of his instrument case. "The Ark is coming to the city of David!"

I smiled at my brother's enthusiasm; I was extremely proud of him. Growing up without our mother had been difficult for us both, and I always felt extra protective of my little brother. But today my heart sang as I witnessed this young man's strong sense of duty and devotion to Almighty God.

"Ever since the king appointed me as a leader of music, I have dreamed of the day when the Ark would rest among our people where it belongs," I told him. "Now, that dream is about to become reality."

As the people gathered by the hundreds, musicians tuning their instruments and singers warming up their voices, it seemed all of Israel was there to witness the event.

David led the procession, his face beaming. He wore the simple linen ephod of a priest, and his joy was infectious. People laughed, clapped, and sang as the Ark, carried on a new cart, made its way down the dusty road from Abinadab's house. The sons of Abinadab —Uzzah and Ahio—walked alongside, guiding the oxen that pulled it.

My fingers itched to play the lyre slung across my back; however, I found myself momentarily distracted by the sight of the Ark itself. It was a vision of divine craftsmanship, its golden surface glinting in the sunlight, the cherubim atop the mercy seat with their wings outstretched as if poised to take flight. The Ark symbolized the very presence of God among His people, and its approach to Jerusalem was nothing short of a moment of triumph for David's reign.

We began to play a jubilant melody that I and the other musicians had composed in preparation for this day. David danced before the Ark, his feet moving in rhythm with the songs of praise, his heart full of worship for the God who had delivered him from his enemies and united the kingdom under his rule.

But then, without warning, disaster struck.

The oxen stumbled as the cart hit a patch of uneven ground. The Ark lurched violently to the side, teetering on the edge of the cart. Uzzah instinctively reached out his hand to steady it.

Instantly, there was a flash of divine power, a shockwave of holiness that stopped the entire procession in its tracks. Uzzah's body went rigid, his outstretched hand touching the Ark for only a second before his lifeless body collapsed to the ground.

A stunned silence fell over the crowd.

I thought my heart would beat out of my chest as I watched David freeze in place, his eyes wide with shock. For a long moment, no one moved. The festive music died in the air, replaced by a crushing weight of dread. The Ark, which had just moments ago been the centerpiece of celebration, now seemed an unbearable source of terror.

David's face twisted in anguish; his joy replaced by fear. He turned away from the scene, his voice hoarse as he called for the procession to halt.

"We cannot continue," he said haltingly. "The Lord's anger has burned against us."

Everyone stood in disbelief as David's men rushed to retrieve Uzzah's body. I could hardly process what had happened. Uzzah had been trying to protect the Ark—yet he had been struck down by the very holiness he sought to preserve. The reality of God's terrifying power settled like a dark cloud over us all.

I noticed my father, whose job it was to protect the Ark, looking bewildered as he surveyed the disturbance.

"Father, do you understand what just happened?" I asked as I ran over to him. My brother soon joined us, looking noticeably pale.

"I am not certain," my father replied. "As Doorkeeper of the Ark, I am responsible for its security and overseeing its respectful transportation. But now look what has happened!"

"Why would God kill Uzzah when we were just trying to honor the Lord?" Zechariah lamented.

"We do not always understand God's ways," my father acknowledged sadly. "But we do know He is faithful, and His ways are beyond anything we could envision."

The three of us stood there for a moment trying to calm ourselves before walking over to the king to await further instructions. David made the decision to have the Ark taken to the house of Obed-Edom, a nearby Levite, where it would remain. The king's plans to bring the Ark to Jerusalem were abruptly put on hold, and the jubilant procession turned into a somber retreat.

Over the next three months, I struggled to reconcile the events of that day. I had always known the Ark was sacred, that it represented the very presence of God. But Uzzah's death had shaken me. It was a harsh reminder of the weight of the holiness the Ark carried, a holiness that demanded the utmost reverence and obedience.

The Ark remained untouched in the house of Obed-Edom, but news spread that his household was being blessed beyond measure. Crops flourished, flocks multiplied, and everything the family put their hands to prospered. The presence of the Ark, it seemed, brought not only danger but also extraordinary blessings.

David's sorrow and fear finally gave way to a renewed determination—but this time, there would be no mistakes. He sought the counsel of the priests and Levites, poring over the Law to understand what had gone wrong. He also consulted with Nathan, a prophet who would become a close friend and trusted adviser, about the proper way to transport the Ark.

One day, I received word that David was ready to try bringing the Ark to Jerusalem again. This time, however, it would not be carried on a cart.

9

THE ARK FINALLY MAKES ITS
WAY HOME

∿

The morning of the second attempt dawned with a sense of quiet reverence. This time, there were no crowds cheering or musicians playing loud and triumphant tunes. The people were more subdued, with a sense of respect that bordered on fear.

The king made it clear that everything would be done according to the Law of Moses. The Ark would be transported by Levites rather than a cart, just as the Lord had commanded. The Levites, including my father and brother, had sanctified themselves for days in preparation for this moment. The poles used to carry the Ark had been carefully placed through the rings on either side, and only the designated Levites would be allowed to touch them.

I stood among the musicians, my lyre in hand, but this time the music would wait until we were sure all was right. I watched as my father and Zechariah, along with the other Levites, approached the Ark with slow, measured steps. They lifted it with the poles, their faces set in solemn concentration, and began the journey toward Jerusalem once again.

At David's command, they took only six steps before stopping. David himself led the sacrifice, offering a bull and a fattened calf as an act of worship and repentance before the Lord. This was no casual procession—it was a sacred act of reverence, a recognition of God's holiness and their need to approach Him with humility and obedience.

When the sacrifice was completed, David broke into a smile and raised his hands in praise. The tension that had gripped the people began to lift, and I felt a wave of relief.

"This time, the Lord has accepted our offering," I exclaimed to the musician standing beside me. "Yes," he agreed, "we now have reason to make a joyful noise."

As the Levites continued carrying the Ark on its journey, the music began again—soft at first, a gentle melody of worship. I plucked the strings of my lyre, my heart filled with a deep sense of honor and respect. The fear I had felt since Uzzah's death was still there, but now it was balanced with a profound understanding of the God we served. He was holy beyond comprehension, yet full of mercy and blessing for those who approached Him in the right way.

David once again danced, but this time his movements were slower, more deliberate. Though he was still delighted, it was tempered by the weight of what we were doing. He wore the same linen ephod as before, but now it was soaked with sweat from his exertions. Yet he did not seem to care—his heart was focused solely on the Lord.

When the Ark finally reached the gates of Jerusalem, the people erupted in celebration. The music swelled into a full chorus, and I played with all my heart, my fingers moving in a flurry of notes. The Levites brought the Ark into the city and placed it in the tent David had prepared.

The king offered more sacrifices, then turned to the people, blessing them in the name of the Lord. He gave every man and woman a loaf of bread, a cake of dates, and a cake of raisins. The city buzzed with excitement as the festivities resumed.

I looked over to where my father was standing near the tent, relief spread across his face. Earlier in the day, as we were making preparations, he was uneasy about this second attempt to transport the Ark. He took his role as Doorkeeper to guard and protect the Ark very seriously, and the disaster on the first endeavor weighed heavily on him.

I gave him a smile before fixing my gaze on the Ark, now resting safely in the heart of Jerusalem. A deep sense of peace settled over me, a peace that came from knowing the Lord was with us—not just as a symbol, but His very presence.

The Ark had finally come to its rightful place, and with it, the worship of Israel would never be the same. I knew the Lord had a purpose for me: *God, You brought me here, to this place, at this time, for a reason,* I prayed. *And I will serve You with all my heart, for as long as it is Your will.*

My friendship with David, once formed in the shadow of a battlefield, now deepened into a bond of shared faith and mission. Collectively, we would bring glory to the God of Israel, whose presence now dwelled among us.

I picked up my lyre once more, the notes flowing freely from my fingers. I began to compose melodies that would echo through the halls of Jerusalem, and into the hearts of God's people, for generations to come.

～

The years following David's ascent to the throne were a whirlwind of political maneuvering, military campaigns, and the establishment of Jerusalem as our nation's center of political and religious power. Now the seat of David's rule and crowned by the Ark of God, the city had also quickly become a regional epicenter of influence.

The most important aspect for me, however, was the evolving relationship I enjoyed with the king. I was extremely pleased that David had not forgotten his roots.

"Do you remember, Asaph, the first time you saw me?" he asked one day as we strolled through the palace garden. "I was but a humble shepherd boy who guarded his father's flocks and composed psalms under the open sky. But the day we met, I had gone up against a giant named Goliath, and the Lord Almighty used me to strike him down."

"I remember that day well, my friend. I was in awe of your words and your deeds. That was the day I pledged to forever be your servant."

David smiled at me fondly. Our shared love for music, for prayer, and for the presence of the Lord further served to solidify our bond. My role in the king's life began to shift from that of a musician in the court to something more intimate and profound.

One evening, after a day of royal duties and meetings with his military commanders, David invited me to his private quarters. The room was modest for a king—sparse, save for a few scrolls, a harp, and an oil lamp flickering in the corner. The weight of the crown seemed to vanish from David when he entered this space. For a moment, he looked like the young shepherd on the battlefield in the Valley of Elah.

"Welcome, my friend," David greeted me warmly, placing his hand on my shoulder. "I have been thinking a great deal about our God, about His faithfulness, and how He has delivered us time and again. We must not let these stories be forgotten. We must sing of His works, so that even our children's children will know the Lord."

I nodded, understanding where the conversation was heading. The psalms David had written in his youth were legendary. But now, as king, David's heart was overflowing with new songs—songs that reflected not only his personal journey but the nation's relationship with God.

"I want you to help me set these to music," David continued, sitting down and reaching for his harp. "Let us make songs that will stir the hearts of the people, songs that will remind them of the God who delivered us from Egypt, who brought us into this land, and who has given us peace."

This was not the first time David had shared his compositions with me. During the years before the Ark's arrival in Jerusalem, we had spent countless hours together working on melodies to accompany David's verses. But now there was a sense of urgency in the king's voice, as if he knew the time was right to bring these songs to life on a larger scale.

David plucked the strings of his harp, a familiar tune I recognized from earlier days. It was a psalm of trust in the Lord, a psalm that spoke of the shepherd's care for his sheep, of the green pastures and still waters that restored the soul.

"The Lord is my shepherd; I shall not want ..." David began singing, his voice rich with emotion.

I listened attentively, allowing the words to wash over me, the imagery vivid in my mind. I could picture the hills of Bethlehem, the quiet nights spent under the stars, and the ever-present sense of God's protection that had carried David through every trial.

I closed my eyes, my fingers moving instinctively over my own lyre, harmonizing with David's voice. The melody grew, taking shape as we worked together, adding layers of sound to reflect the psalm's depth. Hours passed, but neither of us noticed. The music had taken hold of us, and soon we had composed an arrangement that felt timeless—one that would be sung by generations to come.

When the final note faded into the night, David smiled, satisfied but reflective. "This," he said quietly, "is why we were brought together—to remind our people of our God."

I couldn't help but agree. The music we created wasn't merely entertainment or an adornment to royal life. It was worship, a way to draw near to the presence of the Lord and lead others to do the same. I had always felt this way about my role in the tabernacle, but my time together with David that night made it clearer than ever before.

⁓

10

THE LORD'S PROMISE

~

*T*he days that followed were filled with more of the same. David, despite the demands of kingship, set aside time to compose. I often found myself at the king's side, shaping the melodies that would echo in the courts of the Lord. We wrote psalms of lamentation, like those David had penned in the wilderness when he fled from King Saul. We wrote psalms of joy and thanksgiving, celebrating the victories God had given our people over our enemies. And we wrote psalms of repentance, pouring out the sorrow and regret that often accompanied David's reflections on his own sins and failures.

I discovered a deeper understanding and appreciation of music and its power. I learned that a song could be a prayer, a plea, or even a prophecy. The psalms we created were not just for the present day; they were for the future, for times when Israel would need to remember the faithfulness of our God.

One day, David and I were sitting on the rooftop of the palace. David's expression was thoughtful as he looked out over the city of Jerusalem. The sun was setting, casting a golden hue over the buildings and the hills beyond.

"Do you know," David said, his voice soft, "the Lord made me a promise that has never left my mind."

I looked at David curiously. "What promise?"

"That one day, one of my descendants will reign on this throne forever," David replied, looking into the distance as if seeing a vision of what was to come. "A king greater than I could ever be. He will be the true shepherd of Israel ... the Messiah."

The weight of those words hung in the air. I had heard rumors of such a promise, whispers among the priests and Levites, but to hear it from David made it real. The idea that the line of David would bring forth the Messiah, the One who would reign for eternity, was both awe-inspiring and humbling.

"And what will we sing then?" I asked quietly, as if the question were too sacred to ask aloud.

David smiled, his eyes meeting mine.

"We will sing of His majesty, of His righteousness, and of His everlasting kingdom. But for now, we sing of what we know—we sing of the Lord who is our shepherd, who guides us even in the shadow of death, and who prepares a table for us in the presence of our enemies."

≈

As the months passed, the psalms David and I composed began to spread beyond the palace. The Levites sang them before the Ark, the priests chanted them during offerings, and soon the people of Israel took them into their homes. The psalms became a living testament to God's covenant with His people, a bridge between the shepherd king and the God who had anointed him.

My reputation as a musician and psalmist grew alongside David's. I had long been recognized as a talented Levite, but now my name was spoken in the same breath as the king's when it came to worshiping Yahweh. Our melodies filled the streets of Jerusalem, and our songs lifted the hearts of those who heard them.

But for me, the most rewarding part of this journey was not the recognition or the praise. It was knowing I was part of something far greater than myself. I was part of a story that stretched back to the days of Moses, of the Exodus, and of God's covenant with Abraham. And now, through the psalms I wrote with David, I was part of a story that pointed forward—to a time when the Messiah would come and reign in righteousness.

In those quiet moments, as David and I sat with our harps composing songs, I came to understand the true purpose of my calling. It was not just to make music, but to bring the people of Israel into the presence of their God, to remind them of His faithfulness, and to prepare their hearts for the King who was yet to come.

The years passed quickly, and with them came both triumph and sorrow.

One of my greatest joys was marrying a woman named Yehudit, who happened to be the oldest sister of my brother's friend Benesh. Our families had known each other for many years, and the friendship between Yehudit and me eventually grew into something more. She was a beautiful and kind woman who possessed a quiet and gentle spirit. The Lord would go on to bless us with several sons.

David, now a seasoned king, had seen many victories and overcome countless challenges. But as he aged, his thoughts began to turn more and more toward the future—specifically, the future of worship in Israel. The Ark of God rested in a tent in Jerusalem, but David's vision was far grander. He longed to build a permanent house for the Lord, a temple that would befit the greatness of Yahweh and stand as a testament to His faithfulness to Israel.

Those years also marked the fulfillment of much that I had worked toward. The worship before the Ark in Jerusalem had grown into a rich, daily practice, with psalms and music filling the air. Alongside Zechariah and the other musicians, I had seen the power of worship transform the hearts of the people. But even as their music ascended in praise, there was an understanding that something was incomplete. The Ark was still housed in a temporary structure, and the promise of a permanent temple hovered like a prayer yet to be answered.

One evening, David summoned me to the palace. The king's face was lined with age, his hair streaked with gray, but his eyes still held the same fire that had blazed when we were young men. The weight of serving as king had taken an obvious toll, but there was also a renewed sense of purpose.

"Asaph," David said, gesturing for me to sit. "The Lord has been speaking to me about the future."

I sat down, my heart quickening. I had learned to listen carefully whenever David spoke of the Lord's leading.

"You know my heart's desire has always been to build a house for the Lord," David continued, his voice filled with both longing and resignation. "A place where the Ark can dwell, a temple for the God of Israel. But the Lord has made it clear that I will not be the one to build it."

I looked at him, confused. "Why not, my lord? You have served Him faithfully, and there is no one better suited for such a task."

David sighed, his hands resting on the arms of his chair. "It is because I have been a man of war. My hands have shed much blood, and though the Lord has been with me in battle, He desires for the one who builds His house to be a man of peace."

For a moment, neither of us spoke, the only sound the crackle of the fire in the hearth. My mind raced, trying to absorb the significance of David's words. The temple, the very heart of worship in Israel, was to be built by another.

"It will be my son Solomon," David said as if reading my thoughts. "The Lord has promised he will reign in peace, and he will be the one to build the temple."

I nodded slowly. Solomon, though still young, had already shown wisdom beyond his years. He had grown up in the palace, surrounded by the teachings of the Torah and the psalms of his father. But could he carry the weight of such a monumental task?

David once again must have sensed my thoughts, for he smiled and placed a hand on my shoulder. "I know what you're thinking, Asaph. Solomon is young, but the Lord has chosen him. I will make sure he is prepared."

I remained quiet, contemplating the gravity of the moment. I had spent my life serving the Lord in worship, but now I understood the true culmination of my service would not come until the temple was built. And yet, it would not be in my time with David, but in the next generation under Solomon's reign.

~

11

DAVID'S FINAL DAYS

~

*A*fter our conversation, David began pouring his energy into preparations for the construction of the temple. He gathered materials from across the kingdom—cedar from Lebanon, gold, silver, and precious stones. He drew up plans for the structure, working closely with the architects and craftsmen who would bring the vision to life.

I, along with the other worship leaders, was tasked with preparing musical arrangements and the order of worship for the new temple. David wanted to ensure that when the temple was finally built, the worship would be worthy of the Lord's greatness.

The preparations were both exciting and daunting. I often found myself in long meetings with other Levites, discussing how we would organize the shifts of musicians, priests, and gatekeepers once the temple was complete. David's vision was for continual worship before the Lord, with music and prayers filling the temple day and night.

One afternoon, as I sat with Zechariah and the other Levites in the outer courts of the palace, we reviewed the list of musicians who would serve in the temple.

"It's overwhelming, isn't it?" Zechariah remarked, his eyes scanning the scroll in front of him. "This is far greater than anything we've ever done. It's not just about music anymore. It's about creating a legacy."

I nodded as I considered the magnitude of my task. "David's heart has always been for worship," I said thoughtfully. "But what we're doing now will set the standard for generations. The songs we write, the arrangements we create—they will be sung long after we're gone."

Zechariah smiled, though there was a hint of weariness in his eyes. "I suppose that's what it means to serve the Lord, doesn't it? To do something that reaches out beyond your own life."

My brother's words resonated deeply within me. I had always viewed my role as a musician as an act of service to God, but now I saw it in a new light. This temple would stand as a beacon of Israel's relationship with Yahweh, and our music would echo within its walls for centuries.

When David was near the end of his life, he requested the presence of the prophet Nathan and the high priest Zadok.

"You both have been faithful friends and advisers to me for many years," he told them. "Please honor me with this one last request. It is of utmost importance that I name my successor before I die so our nation can continue to function without any disruption. While I am still alive to see it, please take my son Solomon and anoint him as the new king."

Though it saddened the two men to consider someone replacing David, they likewise knew it was unavoidable.

"As you wish, my lord," Nathan responded. "We will see that it is done."

David also called Solomon and the leaders of Israel together for one final act. In a grand assembly, before the priests, Levites, and all the people, David handed over the plans for the temple to Solomon.

"Now, my son, may the Lord be with you and give you success as you follow His directions in building the Temple of the Lord your God," David said, his voice steady despite his age. *"And may the Lord give you wisdom and understanding, that you may obey the Law of the Lord your God as you rule over Israel. For you will be successful if you carefully obey the decrees and regulations that the Lord gave to Israel through Moses. Be strong and courageous; do not be afraid or lose heart!*[1]

"I have prepared everything for you. The materials, the plans, and the instructions. *You have a large number of skilled stonemasons and carpenters and craftsmen of every kind. You have expert goldsmiths and silversmiths and workers of bronze and iron. Now begin the work, and may the Lord be with you!"* [2]

The significance of this exchange between father and son was not lost on me. David, the king who had led Israel through wars, who had united the tribes, and who had brought the Ark to Jerusalem, had now passed the torch to the next generation. And with that torch came the responsibility of building the temple and establishing worship in a way that would honor the God of Israel for all time.

I turned my gaze to Solomon, who stood tall but solemn beside his father. He appeared calm, but there was a tension in his expression, as if the weight of his new role was just beginning to sink in.

When the assembly ended, I found myself standing alone in the quiet of the palace courtyard. I had been with David for so many years—through the battles, the victories, the worship before the Ark. And now, the era of David was ending, and the era of Solomon was dawning: a new temple, a new king, a new chapter in the story of Israel's worship.

I bowed my head and asked the Lord for wisdom for Solomon, for the strength to carry out the immense task before him. And I prayed for myself, that I could continue serving faithfully as we moved into this new season.

The sun began to set, casting a golden light over the city of Jerusalem. I looked out toward the horizon, where the temple would one day stand. It would be a place of glory and splendor; but more than that, it would be a place where the presence of God would dwell among His people.

And though my part in the story was changing, I knew I would be there to help bring it to life.

The stillness in Jerusalem seemed to depress every soul in the city. The sun hung low in the sky, casting an amber glow over the streets and long shadows across the palace courtyard. Word had spread: King David, the beloved ruler of Israel, was nearing the end of his days.

I stood just outside the entrance to the king's chambers, my heart heavy with a grief that had been building for days. Though I had known this moment was coming, nothing could have prepared me for the misery it brought. I had served David for so many years, seen the king at his strongest and his weakest, and I also had counted him as a close friend. To think this chapter was ending left me feeling hollow and distressed, as though the very ground beneath me was shifting.

The palace was silent except for the occasional soft murmur of servants and the rustle of robes as priests and officials moved about quietly.

Solomon had already assumed many responsibilities of the kingdom. But we all knew that as long as David drew breath, a part of Israel's heart remained with him.

I leaned against the cool stone wall and closed my eyes, letting my mind drift back to days gone by. How young we both had been when we first met—David a shepherd with a slingshot, me a Levite with a song in my heart. We had shared so much over the years: victories in battle, psalms of praise and lament, the establishment of Jerusalem as the spiritual and political center of Israel, and the bringing of the Ark to its rightful place. But now it felt as if those years were a fading melody.

I suddenly felt a familiar hand resting on my shoulder, startling me from my thoughts. I turned to see Zadok standing beside me.

"It's time," he said quietly.

I nodded, my throat tight with emotion. I followed Zadok into the king's chambers, where a small gathering had already formed. The room was dimly lit by oil lamps, their soft glow casting flickering shadows on the walls. David lay on a simple bed, his once-strong frame now frail, his breath shallow and labored. The vibrancy that had once defined him seemed to have drained away, leaving only the faintest glimmer of the king who had led Israel through so much.

Solomon stood by his father's bedside, his face grave but composed. He had grown into a man during these past few years, his wisdom already evident in the way he conducted himself. But I could see in his posture that he felt the weight of the kingdom firmly on his shoulders.

David's eyes fluttered open at the sound of footsteps. His gaze shifted toward the figures gathered around him, and a faint smile touched his lips when he saw me.

"My old friend," David whispered, his voice weak but filled with affection.

I stepped closer, kneeling beside the bed. "I'm here, my lord," I said softly, my heart aching at the sight of the once-mighty king now so diminished.

David's hand trembled as he reached for mine. His grip was light, but the connection between us was undeniable.

"You have been a faithful servant, Asaph," David said, his words slow and labored. "Together, we have sung many songs to the Lord."

I swallowed the lump in my throat, forcing myself to keep my composure. "It has been the greatest honor of my life to serve with you," I replied, my voice barely above a whisper.

The king squeezed my hand feebly. "But more than a servant, my friend, you have been a trusted companion all these years. I have indeed been blessed to have you by my side."

"My lord, it is I who has been blessed to be a part of your life—and I will never forget you."

"Asaph, I have one final task to ask of you. Please guide my son as you have always guided me. He still has much to learn and will benefit from your wise counsel. And I know he will need a trustworthy friend."

"I promise to serve Solomon in any capacity he requires," I assured him, my voice breaking.

David's eyes drifted toward the ceiling, as if seeing something far beyond the room. "The Lord ... He has been with me all my days," David said softly, his voice filled with reverence. "From the fields of Bethlehem to the throne of Israel, He has never left my side."

I nodded, my own memories of David's journey flashing through my mind. From the young shepherd boy to the warrior king, David's life had been marked by the presence of God.

But it had also been marked by trials—by the sin with Bathsheba, the rebellion of Absalom, and the countless battles that had worn him down.

David's gaze sharpened for a moment, and he turned his attention to Solomon.

"My son," he said, his voice filled with a father's love and a king's authority. "The Lord has chosen you to build His house. The Temple ... it will be your greatest work."

"I will honor your wishes, Father," Solomon replied earnestly. "The Temple will be built for the glory of the Lord."

David smiled weakly, satisfied. "Be strong, Solomon," he said, his voice fading again. "Lead the people with wisdom. And always, always, follow the Lord."

With that, David's eyes closed once more, his breathing shallow but steady. A hush fell over the room.

I remained kneeling at David's bedside, lost in thought. My grief was overwhelming, but there was also a deep sense of gratitude for the years we had shared. David had not been a perfect man—he had made grave mistakes, and his life had been marked by both victory and tragedy. But through it all, his heart had remained steadfast in its devotion to God. And it was that heart, that passion for worship and for the Lord's presence, that had bound us together all these years.

As the hours passed, the final breaths of King David grew slower and more strained. The soft murmur of prayers filled the room as those gathered whispered words of comfort and scripture, committing David's soul to the Lord.

Then David's chest rose one final time and fell. His body stilled, and the great king of Israel was no more.

∾

12

A NEW ERA

~

A profound silence filled the room as we each absorbed the reality of David's passing. For a moment, it felt as if the very heart of Israel had stopped beating, as if the city itself were holding its breath in mourning our shepherd-king.

Tears welled in my eyes, but I did not allow them to fall. I stood on trembling legs and placed a hand gently on my friend's motionless form.

"May the Lord receive you into His presence, my king," I whispered, my voice thick with emotion.

Zadok stepped forward, his face a mask of grief and reverence. He anointed David's body with oil, a final act of honor for the man who had led Israel for so long. Solomon remained at his father's side, his expression unreadable, though I noticed his clenched jaw and hands.

~

The following days were a blur of ritual and mourning. David's death sent waves of grief through the nation. The streets of Jerusalem echoed with the wails of mourners, and all of Israel seemed to pause to remember the king who had united them and led them well.

I was overcome with my own sorrow, and not even Yehudit could console me. The man I had served for so many years—who had been more than just a king but a friend, a brother in worship—was gone. David's presence, once a constant in my life, had been replaced by a great void.

The funeral procession was a grand affair, befitting our beloved king. David's body was laid to rest in the City of David, his tomb a testament to his legacy. I walked alongside the other Levites and musicians, our steps slow and deliberate as we led the procession with music—psalms of lamentation, songs that David himself had written in moments of sorrow and repentance. The melodies resounded through the streets, a haunting and beautiful tribute to the man who had brought so much music into the heart of Israel.

I couldn't help but notice the faces of the people who lined both sides of the road—men, women, children, their faces etched with grief. David had not just been a king; he had been a symbol of hope, a man after God's own heart. And now, that heart was stilled.

A few days after the funeral, I was alone in the tent where the Ark of God still resided. I had come to this place countless times over the years, leading worship, playing my lyre, singing psalms of praise and thanksgiving. But today, the silence felt heavier than usual. The absence of David was palpable, and for the first time in my life, I felt unsure of what lay ahead.

The majestic Ark stood before me, a reminder of God's faithfulness. But my heart ached as I stared at it. The man who had brought the Ark to Jerusalem, who had danced before it with all his might, had not lived to see his dream of a Temple fulfilled.

I knelt before the Ark, my head bowed, and allowed my unshed tears to finally fall.

"Lord," I whispered, my voice wavering. "What do we do now?"

I wasn't sure if I was asking for myself or for the nation. Without David, it felt as if we had lost our guide, our shepherd. Solomon was wise, yes, but he was young, and the future was uncertain.

In the stillness of that moment, I felt the faintest stirrings of peace. It was not the overwhelming presence of God that had often filled this tent during worship. No, this was a quiet assurance, a reminder that though David was gone, the Lord remained. Israel's hope had never truly been in David—it had always been in Yahweh.

"Thank you, God," I uttered as I wiped my tears and rose to my feet. There was still work to be done. Solomon would need guidance, the Temple was yet to be built, and the songs of Israel's worship would continue. As long as I had breath, I would serve the Lord, just as David had taught me.

But the grief for my friend remained, like a shadow that would never fully leave me. David's death marked the end of an era, a passing of the old ways. I could only pray that the legacy of the man after God's own heart would endure in the days to come.

∼

The day dawned with a sky so clear and blue it seemed as if the heavens themselves had been scrubbed clean in preparation for the event. All of Jerusalem bustled with anticipation. Word had spread throughout the land, and pilgrims from every tribe of Israel had gathered in the city for this monumental occasion—the dedication of Solomon's Temple, the fulfillment of King David's dream, and the heart of Israel's future worship.

I was an old man now, the heaviness of both time and history pressing upon me. I had seen much in my years of service—David's rise to kingship, my own appointment to lead the music before the Ark, the victories and defeats, the joys and the sorrows. But today, this day, felt like the culmination of it all. Solomon's Temple, a vision long dreamed of, now stood before me in its magnificent glory. Every stone, every piece of gold, every intricate carving and engraving spoke of the grandeur and holiness of God.

Many of us had spent countless hours preparing for this day. I, along with my fellow Levites, musicians, and singers, had rehearsed the songs that would praise the Lord when the Ark was brought into the Temple. It was the moment I had lived for—my final offering, perhaps, before my frail body would give way to the years.

I thought back to the day the Ark had been brought to Jerusalem: David leaping before the Ark, the psalms of praise ringing out as the presence of God was carried into the city. But this, the dedication of the Temple, felt like something far greater. It was not only the completion of a promise to David, but also a declaration to the nations that Israel's God, Yahweh, was above all.

～

The streets of Jerusalem were lined with thousands of Israelites, their voices a low hum of excitement. At the center of the grand procession, the

Ark of God was carried by the priests, its golden form glinting in the sunlight. For years, it had been housed in the tent David had pitched, but now its final resting place was in the inner sanctuary of the Temple—the Holy of Holies.

I stood at the head of the musicians with my eyes fixed on the Ark as it moved slowly forward. My heart pounded with a mixture of adoration and wonderment. God's presence felt tangible this day. The Levites and musicians around me held their instruments with a kind of sacred respect, knowing the role they were about to play.

The music began slowly, a single note rising from the shofars, a deep, clear sound that echoed through the streets. It was a call to attention, a summons for all to prepare their hearts. My fingers trembled slightly as I gripped my lyre, waiting for my cue to join in.

"Almighty God," I prayed softly, "I praise You for letting me live to see this day. I am delighted for all of Israel, but I'm especially joyful that King David's vision has been fulfilled."

When the shofars ceased, the cymbals began, a sharp, ringing clash that filled the air. The other instruments followed—harps, lyres, and trumpets blending together in perfect harmony. I lifted my voice with the others, our song rising like incense to the sky.

"Give thanks to the Lord, for He is good! His steadfast love endures forever!"[1]

The words of the psalm, written by David, were familiar, but today they carried a new significance. I could feel the presence of the Lord in our midst. The Ark of God moved forward, step by step, as the music swelled around it. The crowd began to join in, their voices rising with ours.

"Give thanks to the Lord, for He is good! His steadfast love endures forever!"[1]

It was the song of a people who had been delivered from slavery, who had been given a land and a king, and who had now built a house for their God. The sound of it washed over us like a wave; for a moment, I felt as though I were outside of time, part of something eternal. The music, the people, the Ark—all of it was bound together in worship, in the purest offering we could give.

∾

13

THE DEDICATION OF THE TEMPLE

~

*A*s our procession approached the Temple, I looked up at its towering form. The structure was breathtaking. Made of the finest materials, its walls were lined with gold, and its columns rose like mighty trees, strong and majestic. It was a house fit for a king—the King of kings. But even as I marveled at its beauty, I knew the true glory of the Temple was not in its architecture but in the presence of God that would dwell within.

Inside the inner courts of the Temple, the priests prepared for the final act. The Ark of God, the sacred chest that had traveled with Israel since the days of Moses, was brought into the Holy of Holies. Only the high priest, Zadok, would enter that space. I watched as the priests carried the Ark to the steps leading to the inner chamber, the music quieting as they approached the entrance. This was the moment.

The Levites stood in reverent silence, their instruments still, their voices hushed. My breath caught in my throat as Zadok disappeared into the Holy of Holies, the veil falling closed behind him. The silence that followed was almost unbearable. It seemed like all of creation held its breath, waiting for what would come next.

Suddenly, a cloud began to fill the Temple. It started as a soft mist, barely visible, but quickly grew denser until it was impossible to see through. The people fell to their knees as the cloud filled the space, the weight of God's glory descending upon us. It was overwhelming, suffocating in its holiness, yet beautiful in a way that defied words. The presence of the Lord, the Shekinah glory, had come to dwell in the Temple!

I bowed my head, tears streaming down my face. I had known God's presence before, but this was unlike anything I had ever experienced. It was as if heaven itself had opened, and the Lord had come down to be with His people. The majesty and the sanctity of the moment were almost too much to bear.

"Almighty God, thank You for being merciful to Your people," I cried softly. "May we strive each day to do what is right in Your eyes."

For what felt like an eternity, the crowd remained prostrate, their voices silenced by the sheer magnitude of God's glory. My heart was pounding as my trembling hands gripped my lyre. I knew this was the pinnacle, the mountaintop of my spiritual journey. Everything I had done, everything I had sung, every psalm I had composed, had led to this moment. David's dream was fulfilled, and the God of Israel had taken His place in the house built for His name.

Finally, the cloud began to lift, the presence of the Lord receding into the Holy of Holies. The priests and Levites slowly rose to their feet, amazement still etched on their faces. Solomon, who had been standing at the entrance of the Temple, stepped forward to speak. His voice, strong and steady, carried across the courtyard, his words filled with worship and gratitude.

"O Lord, You have said that You would dwell in thick darkness. But I have built a glorious Temple for You, where You can live forever." [1]

As Solomon spoke, I could see the realization of David's promise in the young king's eyes. Solomon had built the Temple, but it was David's heart that had envisioned it. And now, that vision was a reality, a beacon of hope and faith for all of Israel.

The dedication ceremony continued for days, with sacrifices and offerings being made in abundance. Solomon led the people in prayer, and the joy in the city was evident. But for me, the true moment of the dedication had been the descent of God's glory. It was a moment I would carry with me for the rest of my life, a memory that would fuel my worship and my music until my final breath.

As the celebration continued, I savored a quiet moment to myself, standing on the steps of the Temple, looking out over the city of Jerusalem. The sun was beginning to set, casting a golden glow over the rooftops and streets. The sounds of the people—their laughter, their singing, their prayers—drifted up to me, and I smiled.

I knew my time on earth was drawing to a close. My body was frail, my strength waning. But in my heart, I was at peace. I had served the Lord faithfully, and I had seen God's promises to David come to fruition.

As the light faded from the sky, I whispered a prayer of thanksgiving. The Lord had been faithful, and His steadfast love had endured, just as we had sung for so many years.

With one last glance at the Temple, I turned and made my way down the steps, my heart full, knowing that my life had been part of something far greater than myself. I had been a witness to the glory of God … and that was enough.

The music of the Temple, the songs of Israel, would continue long after I was gone. And in those songs, in that worship, my legacy would live on.

~

But as the years passed, the state of our city and its people weighed heavily on my shoulders. My once-strong hands, now knotted with age, rested on my knees as I gazed out over Jerusalem. The city still bustled, but there was something different about it now. The Temple stood in the distance, still gleaming in the sun, but its sacred purpose seemed to have dimmed. The dedication, the glory of God's presence that had once filled the Temple, now felt like a distant memory.

It was not that God had abandoned our people. I knew the Lord's presence was eternal. But the heart of the people—and more grievously, the heart of our king—seemed to have turned away. My prayer that we "strive each day to do what is right in Your eyes" now felt hollow and tainted.

Solomon, the once-promising young king, had slowly but surely shifted his focus. I had attempted numerous times during his reign to offer him fatherly advice, just as I had promised David, but my efforts were rebuffed. Wealth, power, alliances, and a seemingly endless pursuit of knowledge were dominating his reign. And with that, foreign gods had crept into Jerusalem. Once having witnessed the pure joy of Solomon's faith as I served him, I now watched in sorrow as the king's devotion to Jehovah God withered under the allure of the world.

Because of my love and admiration for Solomon's father, I tried once more to render a gentle rebuke for turning away from the teachings of David. I approached him one day at his lavish palace.

"Come in, Asaph," he greeted me warmly. "Why do you look so troubled?"

"My lord, your father considered me to be a close friend and trusted adviser,"

I began, "and I hope I am that to you as well. It grieves me to see you stray from the ways of Jehovah God and be lured by worldly charms. In so doing, not only have you shown contempt for the Lord, but you also have defamed the reputation of one of the great rulers of our time—your father, King David."

I watched as the king's face reddened with rage.

"How dare you speak to me in this manner!" Solomon roared. "Be warned, Asaph. Those who humiliate me are rounded up and executed immediately," he declared. "However, because of your faithful service to my father and his deep love for you, I will not exact the ultimate price for your disrespect.

"But hear me when I tell you this. It would bode well for you to do everything to please this king and gain his favor."

"I meant no disrespect, my lord. I was simply reminding you of your father's deep faith in the God of Israel, and how he depended on the Lord to show him what to do.

"I believe Jehovah God has gifted you the ability to reign justly and carry out your responsibilities honorably if you would only seek His counsel," I continued. "Our people look to you for guidance and will follow where you lead. They know you, my lord; they have watched you grow up. They know you are just as wise as your father, if not more so.

"I beseech you, once more, to seek God as you rule over His people. And I pray He will grant you the courage to accomplish all that is set before you in the days ahead."

With that, I turned and left the palace. I did not know it would be my last conversation with David's son.

On the walk home, I thought back to when Solomon first became king, then began tracing the roots of change. It had begun subtly, almost imperceptibly. Solomon had married women from various nations—Pharaoh's daughter was the first, but others soon followed. These marriages were more than personal unions; they were political alliances. With each new bride, a new god entered Jerusalem.

First, it was whispers of rituals, small idols tucked away in the private quarters of the palace. Then, it became public. Altars to foreign gods appeared on the hills surrounding the city—Molech, Chemosh, Ashtoreth —gods of the very nations Jehovah God had led our people to drive out of the Promised Land.

All of this pained me deeply. The songs of praise I had sung for decades, the worship I had led before the Ark of God, seemed overshadowed by these abominations. I had given my life to the Lord, and now the king, the son of my beloved David, was leading the nation astray.

I wasn't the only one concerned about our future. Other faithful Levites, priests, and elders, including my brother, had begun to complain among themselves. They had hoped Solomon's wisdom—famed throughout the known world—would steer him back to God. But the more he amassed wealth, power, and foreign wives, the more distant Jehovah seemed from the king's heart.

The turning point came when I suffered a personal tragedy—one that would mark my last years with grief.

∼

14

MY BROTHER'S DEATH

~

*T*he day started like any other. I had risen early, kissed my wife farewell, and joined my younger brother to attend to our duties at the Temple. I was grateful that we had remained close throughout the years. Zechariah, always full of life and humor, had been my constant companion in service to the Lord. He also had gone out of his way to help fill the void in my life since David's passing.

While I had taken on more leadership in the music and worship presented before the Ark, Zechariah had managed the daily rituals, ensuring all was done according to the Law. We had shared many moments in the shadow of the Ark, in the quiet of the Temple courts, our voices lifted in song.

But on that morning, there was tension in the air. Rumors had been swirling for weeks—whispers of rebellion and unrest. Solomon's taxes had become oppressive as he sought to fund his lavish lifestyle. The grand palaces he had built, and the tributes he paid to his foreign alliances came at a cost. The people were beginning to grumble, not only about the taxes but also about the king's idolatry. Faithful men of God, like Zechariah, were growing bolder in their public criticism.

"I will not remain silent," Zechariah told me earlier that morning as we prepared for our duties. "The king's sins are leading Israel astray. It's not only our right but our duty to admonish him for his actions."

I attempted to caution him. "Be careful, brother. Solomon is not David. I have spoken to him several times about turning his back on Almighty God, and he did not receive it well. He may not take kindly to rebuke, especially from within the Temple itself."

But Zechariah just shook his head. "If we do not speak out, who will? Our people are suffering, and our God is dishonored by these idols. I fear for what will come if we remain silent."

I shared my brother's concerns; however, a part of me still held out hope Solomon would return to the Lord. Perhaps he could be reasoned with, drawn back by a word of repentance, a call to remember David's covenant with God.

That hope was shattered later that day.

The execution happened swiftly, and the news spread through the Temple courts like wildfire. Zechariah was in the Temple seeing to his responsibilities when a group of armed men, agents of Solomon's court, entered. They moved with purpose, seeking Zechariah out. There was no warning, no trial—only a brutal act of silencing a voice that had dared challenge the king's idolatry.

I was not in the Temple when it happened, but when I arrived, the aftermath greeted me like a knife to the heart. Zechariah's lifeless body lay on the cold, stone floor of the Temple, a pool of blood staining the sacred ground. The sight was too much for me. I dropped to my knees, my heart breaking in ways words could never express.

"Oh dear brother, this cannot be!" I exclaimed as I wept over his body. "Who would commit such an act against a devoted servant of our Lord?" I glanced up at the people scurrying about in the Temple, but not one of them would meet my eye.

How could I possibly continue to perform my duties without my beloved brother by my side?

This was not just a personal loss—it was a sign of the times. The Temple, once the center of Israel's worship, the place where God's glory had descended in a cloud, was now the site of murder. The king, who had been charged with protecting and upholding the law of God, had allowed this atrocity to take place within its sacred walls. In that moment, it felt as if the very foundations of Israel cracked. The city of David was crumbling—not from the outside, but from within.

I cradled Zechariah's body, my tears falling freely now. "I am so sorry I failed you," I whispered to him. "I am the oldest, and it was my responsibility to look out for you and protect you. Please forgive me, little brother."

The days following Zechariah's death were dark. I retreated into my grief, my constant companion. My family tried to comfort me, but it was not to be.

"Asaph, my love, I know you are heartbroken, but remember whom you serve," Yehudit gently reminded me a few days later as I considered returning to the Temple. "You are not serving the king of Israel; you are serving the kingdom of God."

Although I knew my wife was right, it did little to bring me solace in that moment.

I had lost not only a brother but also my faith in Solomon. During the early years of his reign, Solomon had been receptive to my guidance. But the further he drifted from God, the more he had turned his back on me and my counsel. I found it hard to sing, hard to lead the people in worship. *My God, how can I praise You when the king's hands are stained with the blood of my own brother?*

But even in my sorrow, I knew my life was still bound to the service of the Lord. Despite Solomon's fall, despite the corruption that had taken root in the kingdom, my calling had not changed. I had served through David's reign, and I would continue to serve through Solomon's—no matter how unpleasant it became.

Still, the bitterness in my heart grew with each passing day. Solomon, the man chosen by God to build the Temple, was now the cause of Israel's spiritual decline. I watched as the altars to foreign gods multiplied, and the people, once faithful to Jehovah God, began to follow the example of their king. Idolatry spread like a plague, and the holy city of Jerusalem grew more contaminated with each new shrine that appeared.

As I strolled through the outer courts of the Temple one evening, my heart was burdened. The sound of distant sacrifices to foreign gods echoed throughout the city as the sun set behind the hills. Those empty rituals grated against my soul, a constant reminder of how far we, as a people, had fallen.

I stopped at the entrance to the Temple and looked up at its towering columns. The structure was as beautiful as ever, but its purpose seemed meaningless now. The glory that once filled the Temple felt far removed, as if it had departed when the hearts of the people turned away.

I knelt, placing my hands on the cool stone. "How long, oh Lord?" I whispered. "How long will Your people stray? How long will we walk in darkness while the king, the shepherd of Your flock, leads us astray?"

I waited for a response, hoping for some sign, some word from the Lord. But none came. The only sounds were the distant murmurs of the city.

In the quiet, I realized my hope was not in a change of Solomon's heart. It never had been. My hope, my faith, had always been in Jehovah alone. Kings would rise and fall. The hearts of men would grow cold and stray ... but God remained.

With that came a deep resolve. I could not change Solomon's heart. I could not stop the people from following after foreign gods. But I could continue to sing. I could continue to worship, to call out to the Lord, even in the darkness. I could be a voice, small as it might be, that remained faithful in a time of rebellion.

The next day, I returned to my duties. The loss of Zechariah remained with me, the pain still fresh and raw. But as I stood in the Temple, leading the Levites in song, I felt a glimmer of hope. The words of the psalms, the songs of David, still carried power. Even in the midst of decline, even as the nation faltered, the Lord continued to be worthy of praise.

And so I sang. I sang for the people, for the memory of my brother, and for the future generations that would one day return to the Lord. My voice rose above the noise of idolatry and rebellion, a lone cry of faithfulness in a time of great darkness.

> *Truly God is good to Israel,*
> *to those whose hearts are pure.*
> *But as for me, I almost lost my footing.*
> *My feet were slipping, and I was almost gone.*
> *For I envied the proud*
> *when I saw them prosper despite their wickedness.*
>
> *They seem to live such painless lives;*
> *their bodies are so healthy and strong.*
> *They don't have troubles like other people;*

they're not plagued with problems like everyone else.
They wear pride like a jeweled necklace
and clothe themselves with cruelty.
These fat cats have everything
their hearts could ever wish for!
They scoff and speak only evil;
in their pride they seek to crush others.
They boast against the very heavens,
and their words strut throughout the earth.

And so the people are dismayed and confused,
drinking in all their words.
"What does God know?" they ask.
"Does the Most High even know what's happening?"
Look at these wicked people—
enjoying a life of ease while their riches multiply.

Did I keep my heart pure for nothing?
Did I keep myself innocent for no reason?
I get nothing but trouble all day long;
every morning brings me pain.
If I had really spoken this way to others,
I would have been a traitor to your people.
So I tried to understand why the wicked prosper.
But what a difficult task it is!

Then I went into your sanctuary, O God,
and I finally understood the destiny of the wicked.
Truly, You put them on a slippery path
and send them sliding over the cliff to destruction.
In an instant they are destroyed,
completely swept away by terrors.
When You arise, O Lord,
You will laugh at their silly ideas
as a person laughs at dreams in the morning.

Then I realized that my heart was bitter,
and I was all torn up inside.
I was so foolish and ignorant—
I must have seemed like a senseless animal to You.

Yet I still belong to You;
You hold my right hand.
You guide me with Your counsel,
leading me to a glorious destiny.

Whom have I in heaven but You?
I desire You more than anything on earth.
My health may fail, and my spirit may grow weak,
but God remains the strength of my heart;
He is mine forever.

Those who desert Him will perish,
for You destroy those who abandon You.
But as for me, how good it is to be near God!
I have made the Sovereign Lord my shelter,
and I will tell everyone about the wonderful things You do.[1]

≈

15

EVEN IN THE MIDST OF DECLINE

~

*T*he Lord was my shepherd, and though the valley I now walked through was shadowed by grief and loss, I knew God's presence had not left me. The city of David might stumble, and the king himself might fall into wickedness, but my song would rise, lifting the truth of Yahweh above the chaos and despair.

Memories of my earlier years, of David's reign, when the presence of God had been so evident in Jerusalem, sustained me as I walked this difficult path. I remembered the day the Ark of God was brought to the city and the streets were filled with jubilant shouts and songs of praise. I recalled the psalms David had composed—songs of repentance, songs of victory, songs of trust in the God who would establish His kingdom forever. Those psalms had given life to Israel, a people united in worship and faith.

Now, those same psalms became my lifeline. I took comfort in the promises written in the songs I had sung so many times before. The Lord was still my refuge, my strength, a very present help in trouble. I clung to the words that proclaimed God's steadfast love, His faithfulness, and His justice. Though Solomon's actions broke my heart, I knew the truth of the psalms: God's covenant was not with a man or a single generation but with Israel, His people, and it would endure beyond the failures of any king.

One day, as I sat in the Temple courts, I had an idea. My songs could serve as more than a call to worship; they could be a reminder of God's faithfulness and a rebuke to those who had strayed. If Solomon and the leaders of Israel had forgotten the covenant, I could remind them. The psalms could become an anchor for those who still sought to follow Yahweh, a way to hold onto the truth when everything else seemed to falter.

With revived purpose, I called together the musicians and the Levites.

"We will not cease our worship," I told them. "Though the land is filled with idols and the king's heart has wandered, we will continue to sing the songs of David and lift our voices to the Lord. Let the psalms be a light in this darkness, a reminder of who we are and the God we serve."

A number of the Levites, some young and unsure, others seasoned like me, nodded solemnly. They knew the gravity of the times, and they understood the risk of continuing to serve Yahweh in such a climate. But they were also aware their calling was higher than the whims of any king. Their allegiance was to the Lord, the God of Israel, and they would follow Him —no matter the cost.

Together, we resumed our duties with newfound determination. We sang psalms that spoke of God's greatness, His majesty, and His righteousness. My voice, though weathered by age and sorrow, rang out clearly, leading them in worship. The sound of our music filled the Temple courts, and for a moment it felt as though the glory of God's presence had returned—if only in the hearts of those who remained faithful.

As the years continued to roll by, I watched Solomon's reign grow increasingly troubled. The king's relentless pursuit of wealth and power led to greater oppression of the people. The taxes mounted, and Solomon's grand construction projects—including his many palaces—came at the cost of the common folk who toiled under the weight of their king's demands.

In the northern tribes, especially, resentment simmered. The unity David had fought so hard to establish was beginning to unravel. The kingdom, once bound together by faith and worship, was fracturing.

As I prayed alone in my home one evening, I felt the full weight of the years bearing down on me. The vision I had shared with David of a kingdom dedicated to the Lord, where the people walked in righteousness and justice, had faded like a distant dream. And yet, in that moment of doubt, I recalled the promise God had made to David: there would always be a descendant of David on the throne, and one day, an eternal King would come from his line.

It was a promise that transcended Solomon's failures, a promise that spoke of a future beyond the present darkness. I held onto that hope. I believed God's steadfastness would endure, even if the current generation had lost its way.

So, I continued singing psalms that spoke of God's eternal kingdom and His unfailing love. I reminded those around me that though Solomon might have turned away, Yahweh's purposes would still come to pass. My role was to be faithful, to keep the flame of worship alive, and to pass on the truth to the next generation.

I was walking through the city one day when I overheard conversations of discontent. The northern tribes were becoming increasingly vocal about their displeasure with Solomon's rule, and talk of rebellion reached my ears. A chill ran down my spine, realizing their bitterness was only increasing.

"Our king is a hard master," they protested. "Solomon must lighten his harsh labor demands and heavy taxes or face our defiance!"

I thought of my own children and grandchildren, and of the world they would inherit. Would the kingdom split? Would they grow up in a divided Israel, torn by the mistakes of one king?

But I also knew that no earthly kingdom, no matter how glorious, could match the kingdom of God. My hope rested not in the temporary structures of power or the rulers who occupied the throne, but in the eternal promise that David's line would one day bring forth the Messiah.

As I passed the shrines to foreign gods and the palaces built with the people's blood, I whispered a prayer: "Lord, do not let Your people forget. Even in the midst of darkness, keep a remnant that will remain faithful to You. And may Your promise to David endure until the end."

Despite the tragic loss of my brother and the pain of watching the decline of the kingdom I loved, I remained loyal as I continued my work at the Temple. My faith, forged in the fires of suffering, grew stronger. I would hold fast to the Lord, and I would lift my voice in praise until my final breath.

I prayed that my songs, which told the story of God's faithfulness, would sustain future generations—even when human leaders failed. I offered my music as a beacon for those who sought the Lord in times of darkness, a reminder that the God of Israel was still on His throne and that His kingdom would come, even when all seemed lost.

Echoing through the Temple courts, my voice lifted a cry of hope and faith in a God who never abandoned His people. As the music filled the air, I suddenly felt the presence of the Lord, a quiet assurance that even in the midst of decline, God's purposes always prevail.

16

THE KINGDOM FRACTURES

~

*W*ith each new political marriage and each new alliance with foreign nations, Solomon strayed further from the heart of God's covenant. He was consumed with the world and its wealth, its gods, and its pleasures. And the people, once inspired by Solomon's devotion, now saw only their oppression.

As I sat in my courtyard one evening, I listened as some of my fellow Levites spoke in hushed tones about what they had heard. Jeroboam, one of Solomon's trusted officials, was said to be gathering support in the northern regions. The young men spoke of him as a leader of the people, someone who might stand against the king's oppressive policies.

"Revolt is in the air," one of the Levites said quietly. "The northern tribes will not bear these burdens much longer."

Another man agreed. "They say Solomon grows weaker with each passing day, more concerned with his own comfort than the welfare of the people. How much longer before the kingdom tears itself apart?"

I closed my eyes, my heart filled with dread. I had witnessed the days when Israel was united, when the name of the Lord was revered above all, and the people walked in the light of Yahweh's blessing. But now, everything felt fragile, as if the kingdom of Israel—this house that David had built—was crumbling under the strain of Solomon's ambition.

The signs of unrest grew more apparent as the months passed. Delegations from the northern tribes came to Jerusalem, pleading for relief from the heavy taxes and forced labor that had turned their lives into a struggle. The divide between the people and their king was deepening, and there seemed to be no one capable of bridging that gap.

However, the spiritual state of the nation troubled me more than the political turmoil. The foreign gods, once hidden in the private quarters of Solomon's foreign wives, had begun to infiltrate the very fabric of Israelite society. Idolatry was no longer a private sin; it was on display throughout the land. Solomon himself, though still performing the sacrifices in the Temple, no longer held Yahweh above all.

As I walked slowly through the streets of Jerusalem one day, leaning heavily on my staff, I saw an altar to Chemosh on a hill just outside the city. I choked back a sob, my heart sinking as I saw the people—my people —making offerings to a foreign god. I quicky turned away, but the sight stayed with me, a deep wound that festered in my soul.

"Lord, how can this be?" I cried out. "How has it come to this? How have Your people, chosen to be a light to the nations, become so enamored with the gods of those very nations? How has Solomon, the king who built the Temple and asked for Your wisdom, allowed such abominations to take root?"

I felt a familiar pain in my chest, sharp and unrelenting. My physical ailments had worsened in recent years—my heart troubled, my body increasingly frail. I had sought the healing touch of the priests and prayed for relief, but the pain remained. I thought back to the days when I led the Levites in song, my voice lifting high in praise of the Lord. Now, my voice was growing weaker, I was often short of breath, and my body could no longer bear the weight of my grief.

As I lay in bed one evening, struggling to find rest, I reflected on the psalms I had once sung with such conviction. Many of them were the psalms of David, words of hope, trust, and praise for a God who delivered His people from their enemies and established His kingdom forever. I had set those psalms to music, lifting them up in the courts of the Lord, believing with all my heart in the promises they proclaimed.

Now, in the quiet of my room, I wondered if those promises were slipping away. The kingdom of Israel, once united under David, was on the verge of splitting apart. Solomon's sinful ways and oppressive policies had created a spiritual and political fracture that threatened the very foundation of the nation.

I tried to pray, but the words did not come easily. My spirit felt as broken as my body, burdened by the sight of the kingdom I had served my entire life fall into disarray. The God of David's psalms still reigned, I knew, but it was hard to feel that truth when turmoil was all around me.

The next morning, I rose with great difficulty, determined to make my way to the Temple.

"My husband, you should stay home and rest today," Yehudit admonished me. "No one expects a man of your age to continue performing his duties at the Temple every day."

I smiled at my wife and touched her cheek. I had served at the Temple for so many years, leading the people in worship, standing before the Ark of God. Though my body protested every step, I felt compelled to go once more.

"I feel I must make the effort," I told her gently. "My prayer is that God would somehow use my songs to show Solomon the error of his ways."

She nodded, though worry etched her face. She was as heartbroken as I over the way Solomon was ruling our people. The two of us had shared many late-night conversations—and shed many tears—about what David would think of his son's reign.

As I entered the Temple courts, a wave of memories flooded my thoughts. I remembered the joyful celebration the day the Ark had been brought to Jerusalem. I remembered David's songs, the way the king's heart had been so closely knit with Yahweh's. I remembered the day of the Temple's dedication, when Solomon had knelt before the Lord and the glory of Yahweh had filled the house in a cloud.

But now, as I looked around, the Temple seemed tarnished. The presence of the Lord felt distant, obscured by the darkness that had crept into the hearts of my people.

I knelt before the altar, my knees aching from the strain. My breath came in short, labored gasps as I lifted my hands in a prayer that was more a cry of the heart than a well-formed petition.

"Oh Lord," I uttered, my voice barely audible. "How long will Your people stray? How long will this kingdom be divided? Remember Your covenant with David, and have mercy on Your people. Turn their hearts back to You, Lord, before all is lost."

I stayed there for a long time, my heart heavy, my body weak. But even in my lament, I held on to a small flicker of hope. I still believed in the faithfulness of Yahweh, and I still believed in His promises.

In the months to come, the northern tribes, led by Jeroboam, began threat-ening rebellion. Solomon, now isolated and consumed by his own pursuits, seemed either unwilling or unable to address the growing crisis. The kingdom was splintering, just as I had feared—and I couldn't help but feel as if we all had disappointed our beloved King David.

After Yehudit and I retired to bed one evening, the pain in my chest grew more intense as I considered what was happening. But as my breath grew shallow and my vision dimmed, I clung to the words I had sung so many times before: *"The Lord is my shepherd; I shall not want."*[1]

Even in the valley of the shadow of death, I knew the Lord was with me. And as the darkness closed in, my final prayer was not for myself but for Israel—that the God of David, the God who had delivered His people so many times before, would once again have mercy on them, and that His promise would endure, even beyond the coming split of the kingdom.

∾

17

ONE FINAL PSALM

~

*T*hose tending to me moved quietly around the courtyard, aware that my health was fragile. My chest ached constantly now, a dull, unrelenting pain that reminded me of my mortality. Still, despite my physical decline, my spirit wrestled with the deep questions of my life and the condition of the kingdom.

I closed my eyes, letting the past come flooding back to me.

Now, as an old man, I could see the full arc of my life. From the hope of David's kingdom to the disillusionment of Solomon's reign, from the heights of worship to the depths of grief, my life had been a long, winding journey of faith. Yet through it all, there had been one constant: the devotion of Yahweh.

I reached out and took up my lyre, my trembling fingers caressing the strings as I thought of the psalms I had sung so many times before. They had been the songs of a younger man, filled with hope and trust in the Lord's deliverance. Now, as my life neared its end, I felt the need to compose one final psalm—a lament for the state of Israel, for the broken-ness of the kingdom, and for my own journey of sorrow and faith.

"O Lord, where is the light of Your face?
Once we danced before You,
Once our voices lifted high the sound of Your praise.
But now, O God, the earth is silent,
And the songs of Zion grow faint.
You brought us out of bondage,
You set our feet on the holy hill,
Yet we have turned away.
Our hearts have gone astray to other gods,
And the glory of Your house is dimmed.

O Lord, remember the days of David,
When Your servant ruled in righteousness,
And the people walked in Your ways.
Remember the promise You made, O Lord,
That David's line would never fail.
But now the kingdom trembles,
And the hearts of Your people are far from You.

The altars of foreign gods stand high,
And the cries of the poor go unheard.
How long, O Lord, will You hide Your face?
How long will You turn away from Your people?
We are weak, our strength has failed,
And the oppressor grows strong in the land.

But I will trust in Your unfailing love,
I will hope in Your covenant forever.
For though the darkness may cover the earth,
Your light will shine again,
And Your name will be praised in all the land.

Deliver us, O Lord, and have mercy on Your people.
Remember Your servant David, and the promise You made.
Let Your kingdom come, let Your will be done,
In Israel, as it is in heaven."

My voice trembled as I sang those final words that would never be published in the collection of Psalms. It was a cry from the depths of my soul, a lament for all that had been lost; yet, a declaration of trust in the God who never failed. I knew my time had come to an end, but I would leave this world with the assurance that Yahweh's promises would endure, even if I did not live to see them fulfilled.

The night was quiet, a deep stillness settling over Jerusalem as I lay on my bed, my breathing shallow and labored. My body had grown so weak I could no longer rise without assistance, but in my heart, I felt a strange peace. The pain that had once gripped me seemed to ease, and I suddenly felt the presence of the Lord closer than ever.

My wife, children, and grandchildren gathered around me, their faces lined with sorrow. But I felt no fear; my time had come, and I was ready. I had served Yahweh faithfully all my life, and though the kingdom was in peril, though Solomon had failed, I knew God would not fail.

My mind drifted to the days of my youth, to the sound of David's voice as we sang together in the courts of the Lord. I could hear the psalms again, their melodies rising in my mind like a distant echo.

As my breathing slowed, I felt a warmth surround me, a gentle presence that seemed to carry me beyond the pain and sorrow of this world. My heart, once troubled, now beat with a quiet assurance.

And then, with one final breath, I was gone.

⁓

PLEASE HELP ME BY LEAVING A REVIEW!

i would be very grateful if you would leave a review of this book. Your feedback will be helpful to me in my future writing endeavors and will also assist others as they consider picking up a copy of the book.

To leave a review:

Go to: amazon.com/dp/195686640X

Or scan this QR code using your camera on your smartphone:

Thanks for your help!

~

YOU WILL WANT TO READ ALL THE BOOKS IN "THE CALLED" SERIES

Stories of these ordinary men and women called by God to be used in extraordinary ways.

A Carpenter Called Joseph (Book 1)

A Prophet Called Isaiah (Book 2)

A Teacher Called Nicodemus (Book 3)

A Judge Called Deborah (Book 4)

A Merchant Called Lydia (Book 5)

A Friend Called Enoch (Book 6)

A Fisherman Called Simon (Book 7)

A Heroine Called Rahab (Book 8)

A Witness Called Mary (Book 9)

A Cupbearer Called Nehemiah (Book 10)

A Follower Called Mark (Book 11)

A Psalmist Called Asaph (Book 12)

AVAILABLE IN PAPERBACK, LARGE PRINT, AND FOR KINDLE ON AMAZON.

ALSO, A **DISCUSSION GUIDE** IS AVAILABLE AS A RESOURCE **FOR YOUR SMALL GROUP OR BOOK CLUB** AS YOU DISCUSS EACH OF THE BOOKS. AVAILABLE ON AMAZON IN PRINT OR FOR YOUR KINDLE.

Scan this QR code using your camera on your smartphone to see the entire series.

"THE PARABLES" SERIES

An Elusive Pursuit (Book 1)

Twenty-three year old Eugene Fearsithe boarded a train on the first day of April 1912 in pursuit of his elusive dream. Little did he know where the journey would take him, or what . . . and who . . . he would discover along the way.

Available on Amazon

~

A Belated Discovery (Book 2)

Nineteen year old Bobby Fearsithe enlisted in the army on the fifteenth day of December 1941 to fight for his family, his friends, and his neighbors. Along the way, he discovered just who his neighbor truly was.

Available on Amazon

~

AVAILABLE IN HARDCOVER, PAPERBACK, LARGE PRINT, AUDIO, AND FOR KINDLE ON AMAZON.

Scan this QR code using your camera on your smartphone to see the entire series.

For more information, go to *kenwinter.org* or *wildernesslessons.com*

ALSO BY KENNETH A. WINTER

THROUGH THE EYES

(a series of biblical fiction novels)

Through the Eyes of a Shepherd (Shimon, a Bethlehem shepherd)

Through the Eyes of a Spy (Caleb, the Israelite spy)

Through the Eyes of a Prisoner (Paul, the apostle)

∿

THE EYEWITNESSES

(a series of biblical fiction short story collections)

For Christmas/Advent

Little Did We Know – the advent of Jesus — for adults

Not Too Little To Know – the advent – ages 8 thru adult

For Easter/Lent

The One Who Stood Before Us – the ministry and passion of Jesus — for adults

The Little Ones Who Came – the ministry and passion – ages 8 thru adult

∿

LESSONS LEARNED IN THE WILDERNESS SERIES

(a non-fiction series of biblical devotional studies)

The Journey Begins (Exodus) – Book 1

The Wandering Years (Numbers and Deuteronomy) – Book 2

Possessing The Promise (Joshua and Judges) – Book 3

Walking With The Master (The Gospels leading up to Palm Sunday) – Book 4

Taking Up The Cross (The Gospels – the passion through ascension) – Book 5

Until He Returns (The Book of Acts) – Book 6

ALSO AVAILABLE AS AUDIOBOOKS

THE CALLED series

A Carpenter Called Joseph

A Prophet Called Isaiah

A Teacher Called Nicodemus

A Judge Called Deborah

A Merchant Called Lydia

A Friend Called Enoch

A Fisherman Called Simon

A Heroine Called Rahab

A Witness Called Mary

A Cupbearer Called Nehemiah

A Follower Called Mark

A Psalmist Called Asaph

∾

THROUGH THE EYES series

Through the Eyes of a Shepherd

Through the Eyes of a Spy

Through the Eyes of a Prisoner

∾

Little Did We Know

Not Too Little to Know

∾

THE PARABLES series

An Elusive Pursuit

A Belated Discovery

SCRIPTURE BIBLIOGRAPHY

~

The basis for the story line of this book is taken from *the books of First Samuel, Second Samuel, First Kings and Psalms* in the Holy Bible. Certain fictional events or depictions of those events have been added.

Some of the dialogue in this story are direct quotations from Scripture. Here are the specific references for those quotations:

Chapter 1

[1] Exodus 25:8-9

[2] 1 Samuel 4:22

[3] 1 Samuel 6:20

Chapter 2

[1] Judges 5:24

[2] Judges 6:12

[3] Judges 6:13

[4] Judges 6:14

(5) Judges 6:15

(6) Judges 6:16

(7) Judges 6:36-37

(8) Judges 6:39

(9) Judges 7:2-3

(10) Judges 7:4

(11) Judges 7:5

(12) Judges 7:7

Chapter 3

(1) 1 Samuel 7:3

(2) 1 Samuel 7:8

(3) 1 Samuel 7:12

(4) 1 Samuel 8:5

(5) 1 Samuel 8:7-9

(6) 1 Samuel 8:11-18

Chapter 4

(1) 1 Samuel 9:6

(2) 1 Samuel 9:7

(3) 1 Samuel 9:8

(4) 1 Samuel 9:11

(5) 1 Samuel 9:12-13

(6) 1 Samuel 9:16

(7) 1 Samuel 9:17

(8) 1 Samuel 9:18

(9) 1 Samuel 9:19-20

(10) 1 Samuel 9:21

(11) 1 Samuel 9:27

(12) 1 Samuel 10:1-8

(13) 1 Samuel 10:11

(14) 1 Samuel 10:12

(15) 1 Samuel 10:18-19

(16) 1 Samuel 10:22

(17) 1 Samuel 10:22

(18) 1 Samuel 10:24

(19) 1 Samuel 10:24

Chapter 5

(1) 1 Samuel 15:11

(2) 1 Samuel 17:8-10

Chapter 6

(1) 1 Samuel 17:28

(2) 1 Samuel 17:29

(3) 1 Samuel 17:34-36

(4) 1 Samuel 17:37

(5) 1 Samuel 17:37

(6) 1 Samuel 17:43-44

(7) 1 Samuel 17:45-47

Chapter 7

(1) 1 Samuel 18:7

(2) Psalm 78:70-71

Chapter 11

[1] 1 Chronicles 22:11-13

[2] 1 Chronicles 22:15-16

Chapter 12

[1] Psalm 107:1

Chapter 13

[1] 1 Kings 8:12-13

Chapter 14

[1] Psalm 73

Chapter 16

[1] Psalm 23:1

∾

LISTING OF CHARACTERS (ALPHABETICAL ORDER)

∽

Many of the characters in this book are real people pulled directly from the pages of Scripture. I have not changed any details about a number of those individuals except the addition of their interactions with the fictional characters. They are noted below as "UN" (unchanged).

In other instances, fictional details have been added to real people to provide backgrounds about their lives where Scripture is silent. The intent is that you understand these were real people, whose lives were full of all of the many details that fill our own lives. They are noted as "FB" (fictional background).

In some instances, we are never told the names of certain individuals in the Bible. In those instances, where i have given them a name as well as a fictional background, they are noted as "FN" (fictional name).

Lastly, a number of the characters are purely fictional, added to convey the fictional elements of these stories. They are noted as "FC" (fictional character).

∽

Aaron – brother of Moses, first high priest of Israel (Levite) (UN)
Abiel – son of Zeror, father of Kish (Benjaminite) (UN)

Abiezer – clan of Manasseh to which Joash belonged (UN)

Abinadab – owner of household at which the Ark resided after it was returned by the Philistines (Levite) (UN)

Abner – King Saul's general (Benjaminite) (FB)

Ahio – grandson of Eleazar, caretaker of the Ark at the household of Abinadab (Levite) (UN)

Aphiah - ancestor of King Saul (UN)

Asaph – son of Berechiah, husband of Yehudit, chief minister before the Ark, leader and writer of music under Kings David and Solomon (Levite) (FB)

Ashtoreth – pagan goddess of Philistines (UN)

Baal – pagan god of Philistines (UN)

Balaam – prophet of Midian, attempted to seduce the Israelites away from Jehovah God for hire (Midianite) (UN)

Balak – king of Moab, defeated by Ehud (Moabite) (UN)

Barak – son of Abinoam, student under Shamgar, commander of Israel's army under Deborah (Naphtalite) (FB)

Becorath - ancestor of King Saul (UN)

Benesh – friend of Zechariah, brother of Yehudit (FC)

Berechiah – son of Shimea, father of Asaph, gatekeeper for the Ark in Abinadab (Levite) (UN)

Bezalel - son of Hur, skilled craftsman (UN)

Chemosh - a pagan Moabite god (UN)

David – son of Jesse, shepherd, second king of Israel (Judahite) (FB)

Deborah – daughter of Oded, wife of Lappidoth, fourth judge over Israel (Benjaminite) (FB)

Eleazar – son of Abinadab, initial caretaker of the Ark in his father's household (Levite) (FC)

Eli – high priest of Israel (Levite) (UN)

Eliab – son of Jesse, older brother of David (Judahite) (FB)

Gershon – eldest ancestral son of Levi (Levite) (UN)

Gideon – son of Joash, husband of Alya, fifth judge of Israel (Manassehite) (FB)

Goliath – giant from Gath, defeated by David (Philistine) (FB)

Heber – youngest son of Abdon, husband of Jael (Kenite) (FB)

Hobab – son of Jethro, Moses's wife's brother (Midianite) (UN)

Jabin – son of King Tirshi, king of Hazor, defeated by Barak (Hazorite) (FB)

Jael – wife of Heber, mother of baby son Joseph, killed Sisera (Kenite) (FB)

Jair – judge of Israel (Gileadite) (UN)

Jeroboam - first king of the northern kingdom of Israel, son of Nebat (UN)

Jethro – father-in-law of Moses, prince and priest of Midian (Midianite) (UN)

Joash – father of Gideon, presented dispute before Deborah (Manassehite) (FB)

Jonathan - son of King Saul (UN)

Joseph – baby son of Jael (Kenite) (FC)

Joshua - son of Nun, chosen by God to lead His people into the Promised Land (UN)

Kish – son of Abiel, grandson of Zeror, father of Saul (Benjaminite) (UN)

Levi - son of Jacob (Israel), father of Gershon (UN)

Michael – a Levite, a descendant of Gershon, son of Baaseiah, great-grandfather of Asaph (Levite) (FB)

Molech - a Canaanite god that demanded the sacrifice of children (UN)

Moses – an adopted prince in the palace of Egypt, a shepherd in Midian, led Israelites out of Egypt and through the wilderness (Levite) (UN)

Nahash – king of Ammon (Ammonite) (UN)

Nathan – prophet of Jehovah God sent to David (Ephraimite) (FB)

Nebat - father of Jeroboam (UN)

Noya – younger daughter of Deborah and Lappidoth, wife of Zeror, great grandmother of King Saul (Ephraimite) (FC)

Obed-edom - the Gittite, owner of the threshing floor where the Ark remained for three months (UN)

Phinehas - son of Eli (the high priest) (UN)

Purah – Gideon's servant and armor bearer (Manassehite) (UN)

Rachel – wife of Berechiah, mother of Asaph and Zechariah, died in childbirth (Levite)
(FB)

Samson – son of Manoah, judge of Israel (Danite/ Nazirite) (UN)

Samuel – son of Elkanah, given to the Lord by his mother Hannah, raised in Shiloh in the house of Eli, prophet and last Judge of Israel (Ephraimite) (FB)

Saul – son of Kish, first king of Israel (Benjaminite) (FB)

Shimea – son of Michael, grandfather of Asaph, born in Kedesh (Levite) (FB)

Sisera – general over Hazorite army, during Jabin the 2nd's rule (Sardinian) (FB)

Solomon – son of David, third king of Israel (Judahite) (FB)

Tola – son of Puah, judge of Israel (Issacharite) (UN)

Tzipora – daughter of Jethro, Midianite princess, wife of Moses (Midianite) (UN)

Uzzah – grandson of Eleazar, caretaker of the Ark at house of Abinadab, died when he reached out his hand to steady the Ark when it was about to fall (Levite, but not Gershonite) (FB)

Yehudit – wife of Asaph (Ephraimite) (FC)

Zadok – high priest during the reign of David (Levite) (UN)

Zechariah – son of Berechiah, younger brother of Asaph, a singer who sounded bronze cymbals (Levite) (FB)

Zeror – son of Bechorath and Noya, father of Abiel (Benjaminite) (FB)

∼

ACKNOWLEDGMENTS

I do not cease to give thanks for you ....
Ephesians 1:16 (ESV)

… my partner and best friend, LaVonne,
for choosing to trust God as we have walked together with Him through
this faith adventure from beginning to end;

… my family,
for your continuing love, support, and encouragement throughout it all;

… Sheryl,
for your partnership and collaboration in this work;

… Scott,
for the heart and giftedness from God you have once again expressed
through the cover design of this book, my brother;

… a precious group of advance readers,
who have encouraged and challenged me throughout my writing journey;

… and most importantly,
to the One who enabled the completion of this book,
even when it didn't seem possible—the One upon whom we are all
desperately dependent—the One who goes before us in all things
– my Lord and Savior Jesus Christ!

∾

EDITOR'S NOTE

≈

I first met Ken many years ago when he served as one of my vice presidents at the International Mission Board (IMB) in Richmond, Virginia until 2015. Leadership's dissolution of the IMB Communications Department in 2016 scattered about fifty employees far and wide, including me. I moved back to my hometown of Lynchburg and began working for another nonprofit Christian organization. Unfortunately, I lost touch with the majority of my IMB family.

When COVID struck in 2020, I suddenly found myself unemployed yet again; ironically, my husband lost his job the day after I lost mine. As the two of us prayed and worried over our circumstances, I received a phone call from Ken asking if I'd be interested in editing a book manuscript he'd just written. I don't think we'd even been in contact during those years since leaving the IMB. Was his call a coincidence? I think not.

Ken was unaware God was using him to answer my prayer: *Should I try to go out on my own?* His phone call gave me the courage to dip my toe into the world of freelance editing. That first book was the launch of a cherished, personal relationship as we worked together to honor Christ through the telling of numerous stories about men and women of the Bible.

I have heard the word "sacred" used to describe the relationship between a writer and his editor. It is certainly one based on absolute trust as a writer is at his most vulnerable, allowing another person to critique and change his words.

Thank you, my friend, for trusting me to take this journey with you. Your words have inspired and challenged me in my own spiritual walk. I have no doubt that the day God calls you home, the first words you hear are: "Well done, my good and faithful servant."

Sheryl Martin Hash

∼

FROM THE AUTHOR

A word of explanation for those of you who are new to my writing.

You will notice that whenever i use the pronoun "I" referring to myself, i have chosen to use a lowercase "i." This only applies to me personally (in the Preface). i do not impose my personal conviction on any of the characters in this book. It is not a typographical error. i know this is contrary to proper English grammar and accepted editorial style guides. But years ago, the Lord convicted me – personally – that in all things i must decrease and He must increase. And as a way of continuing personal reminder, from that day forward, i have chosen to use a lowercase "i" whenever referring to myself.

Because of the same conviction, i use a capital letter for any pronoun referring to God. The style guide for most translations of Scripture do not share that conviction. However, you will see that i have intentionally made that slight revision and capitalized any pronoun referring to God in any quotations of Scripture. Please accept my apology for any style guide violations , but i must honor this conviction.

Lastly, regarding this matter – this is a <u>personal</u> conviction – and i share it only so you will understand why i have chosen to deviate from normal editorial practice. i am in no way suggesting or endeavoring to have anyone else subscribe to my conviction. Thank you for your understanding.

∼

ABOUT THE AUTHOR

Ken Winter is a follower of Jesus, an extremely blessed husband, and a proud father and grandfather – all by the grace of God. His journey with Jesus has led him to serve on the pastoral staffs of two local churches – one in West Palm Beach, Florida and the other in Richmond, Virginia – and as the vice president of mobilization of an international missions organization.

Today, Ken continues in that journey as a full-time author, teacher and speaker. You can read his weekly blog posts at kenwinter.blog and listen to his weekly podcast at kenwinter.org/podcast.

And we proclaim Him, admonishing every man and teaching every man with all wisdom, that we may present every man complete in Christ. And for this purpose also I labor, striving according to His power, which mightily works within me.
(Colossians 1:28-29 NASB)

PLEASE JOIN MY READERS' GROUP

Please join my Readers' Group in order to receive updates and information about future releases, etc.

Also, i will send you a free copy of *The Journey Begins* e-book — the first book in the *Lessons Learned In The Wilderness* series. It is yours to keep or share with a friend or family member that you think might benefit from it.

It's completely free to sign up. i value your privacy and will not spam you. Also, you can unsubscribe at any time.

Go to kenwinter.org to subscribe.

Or scan this QR code using your camera on your smartphone:

∼

www.ingramcontent.com/pod-product-compliance
Lightning Source LLC
Chambersburg PA
CBHW072357190626
46811CB00019B/1203